tales from THE HANGING MONKEY

AIRSHIP 27 PRODUCTIONS

AN AIRSHIP 27 PRODUCTION

Tales from the Hanging Monkey–Volume 1

THE DEVIL'S CRATER © 2012 by Joshua Reynolds
THE EYE OF KA © 2012 by Bill Craig
MOTUGRA'S REVENGE © 2012 by Tommy Hancock
THE KNOBLOCH COLLECTION ASSIGNMENT © 2012 by Derrick Ferguson

Published by Airship 27 Productions
www.airship27.com
www.airship27hangar.com

Interior illustrations © 2012 Clayton Hinkle
Cover illustration © 2012 Daniel Ibanez

Editor: Ron Fortier
Associate Editor: Ray Riethmeier
Production and design by Rob Davis.

ISBN-13: 978-0615653006
ISBN-10: 0615653006

Printed in the United States of America

10 9 8 7 6 5 4 3 2 1

tales from
THE HANGING MONKEY

Table of Contents

Corky O'Brian

Khuna

Miko

Nick Fortune

Grace Thomas

Jimmy Dolan

THE DEVIL'S CRATER

By
Joshua Reynolds

"**M**r. Dolan? Jimmy Dolan?"

The rain outside the Hanging Monkey was loud, and the music inside was louder, but Jimmy Dolan heard the woman's voice just fine. Selective hearing in action, as Corky O'Brian, the joint's owner, called it. Jimmy straightened from his shot, resting the pool cue on his shoulder, and turned, beaming.

"Who's asking?" he said. Then, quickly, "How about a drink?"

"I–no. No thank you. Are you Jimmy Dolan?" The speaker was taller than average, with the rangy, raw-boned look that some women from the Midwestern United States had. Blonde hair, pulled back tight in a single, coiled braid, showed off the strong face and Swedish blue eyes. Jimmy looked her up and down, grinning.

"Could be. Does he owe you money? Child support?"

"Hardly." She sniffed and returned the favor, her eyes roaming over him. Dolan didn't mind. He was just a hair under six feet, and dressed for business and comfort in khaki. A baby face and curly blonde hair completed the picture. The woman didn't seem to like what she saw despite that, which caused Jimmy's smile to falter just a bit.

"I'm Dolan," he said, after a moment of awkward silence. "And you are…?"

"Orne. Sonia Orne." She held out a hand. Jimmy stared at it for a moment, then took it, bent low and swept his lips lightly over her knuckles. She jerked her hand back and he straightened, grinning.

"What? Too soon?"

"Definitely," she said, rubbing the back of her hand on her trousers. "I understand you have a plane?"

"Eight-seater. Grumman Goose, the *Lucy Goosey*. What do you need transported?"

"Me. And four other people." Orne held up five fingers for emphasis.

Jimmy scrubbed his palm across his stubbled chin.

"I don't usually take passengers."

"No? Then perhaps I've come to the wrong pilot," Orne said. She turned as if to leave, and Jimmy extended his pool cue, blocking her path.

"I said I usually don't take passengers. Not that I wouldn't."

"What are your rates?" she said, turning back around. Jimmy grinned.

"More than fair. Want to discuss it over a drink?" Jimmy tossed his pool cue onto the table and made a 'see ya' gesture to his grinning opponent.

"If you insist."

Jimmy led her towards the bar. The Monkey was crowded this time of evening, especially given the weather outside. Rain ran in waves down the clapboard and bamboo walls, and did a tap-dance across the shingles on the roof. Behind the bar, an Asian woman slung drinks with brisk efficiency.

"Miko! Two Sliders," Jimmy said, knocking on the bar and holding up two fingers. Orne sat beside him, frowning.

"You don't even know what I want," she said.

"Trust me. You'll love this," he said, turning his back to the bar and plopping his elbows down on it. "Corky—the guy who owns this joint—came up with this drink that's...thanks, Miko." He interrupted himself as the bartender slid two dark drinks towards he and Orne. Dolan scooped them up and handed one to Orne. "Down the hatch, m'lady."

Orne began to cough even as the drink touched her tongue. "God, what is that?"

"Cough syrup," Jimmy said knocking back his. "Either that or the motor oil. Gives it a real kick, right?"

"Horrible," Orne said, pushing the glass away. "God."

"Hey, I'll have yours then. Wouldn't want to insult Miko." Jimmy nodded to the woman behind the bar.

"Japanese name." Orne said it in a measured tone.

"Chinese lady." Jimmy shrugged. "No clue, so don't ask. She's touchy about it, and I've seen her put a fist through four inches of wood, so don't expect me to ask either." He grabbed Orne's glass and tipped it back. Wiping his mouth, he eyed her. "Okay. Details, if you please."

"Can I ask your price?"

"Depends on the details."

"Five people. We need to go to Ghora." Orne hunched forward, her eyes swiveling as if she expected eavesdroppers to be dropping eaves left and right. "Do you know it?"

Jimmy said nothing for a moment. Then, "No."

"What?"

"No. Actually, hell, no."

"What?" Orne blinked as Jimmy hopped off his bar stool. He glanced at her.

"Ghora? You have got to be kidding." He shook his head. "What possible reason could you have for going to that slice of jolly green hell?"

"To possibly save a man's life." Orne's eyes flashed. Jimmy hesitated, then sighed.

"Go on."

"I'm a graduate student. Miskatonic University. You've heard of it?"

"No."

"Then you're even more uncultured than I thought. We have the top anthropology and archaeology departments in the Western Hemisphere. Professor Freeborn—my boss—has forgotten more about the potential origins of our species than Darwin ever even suspected."

"Fascinating. What does that have to do with saving somebody's life?" Jimmy said.

"Professor Freeborn went to Ghora last year. He was doing research on the ritual practices of the tribes that live on the slopes of the Ghoral Crater—you know of it?"

"Yeah. It's a volcano, only it ain't active. You can see it from the air."

"We lost contact with him six months ago. It's taken us this long to get the necessary permits and permissions to organize a second expedition." She gestured helplessly. "We need to get to Ghora as quickly as possible. To see if Professor Freeborn is—is...." Her throat bobbed and Jimmy could see that she was fighting to stay in control.

"Guy means a lot to you, hunh?" he said, taking her arm and leading her towards a quiet table at the back of the bar. Two men were already sitting there, but they got up as Jimmy indicated Orne and gestured to her face. Orne sat down without noticing the exchange.

"He was a good teacher," she said, after a moment.

"Was?"

"Is," she said more firmly. "He's alive. I know it."

Jimmy sat back in his chair. He chewed his lower lip for a moment, then quoted a price. Orne blinked.

"That's—"

"All inclusive. For that price you get a guide as well as a pilot, not to mention security." He knocked on the table.

"A—a guide?"

"Well, yeah, babe," Jimmy said. "What? You thought I was going to land you *on* the crater?"

"But-did you just call me babe?"

"Sorry. Ms. Orne," Jimmy said. "Look, I know Ghora."

"You said you didn't!" Orne sputtered.

"I said I wasn't *going* to Ghora, not that I didn't know it." Jimmy held up his hand. "You're going to need a guide. I happen to know a guide. All inclusive, like I said."

Orne leaned back in her seat. "Fine." She held out her hand. Jimmy took it.

"Tomorrow. First light. You be ready by then?"

"I think we can manage." She smiled crookedly. "Thank you."

"Don't thank me yet." Jimmy looked up at her as she stood. She walked out of the bar a few moments later, leaving him staring after her.

Someone joined him at the table. "You're a sap," Corky O'Brian said. O'Brian was an ex-prizefighter and an Irish Republican of the old style. His face looked as if it had gone three losing rounds with a sledgehammer, but his eyes shone with good humor. "A grade-A sap, Dolan."

"Shaddap," Jimmy said, not looking at him.

"Seriously. Ghora?" The owner of the Hanging Monkey slapped a hand on the table. "That island eats people."

"Technically, it's just the people who live on the island who eat people."

"Were you going to tell her that?"

"I assume she knows." Jimmy rubbed his chin. "I wonder if this Freeborn guy got eaten."

"Probably," Corky said, shrugging. "That change things?"

"Not for me." Jimmy looked at the other man. "I need to borrow Khuna."

"What? Why?" Corky glanced over at the Hanging Monkey's wiry bouncer. Khuna was a Motugran, and fiercely loyal to the Irishman for reasons that neither man felt like sharing. Small, compact and pantherish, the islander sported an outfit that was equal parts cultural costume and military uniform. A rifle bandolier was slung across his tattooed chest, studded with ammunition, animal teeth and thin knives, and his feet were bare. He sat on the edge of the bar, whittling a length of whitish bone.

"He's been to Ghora, right?" Jimmy said.

Corky frowned. "Probably. His people took heads all through these islands up until a few years ago."

"So," Jimmy said, gesturing. "I need him to act as guide for this little expedition."

"No."

"Why?"

"I need him here. Who's going to toss troublemakers if Khuna's not here?"

Jimmy shrugged. "Miko."

"Miko is a delicate flower and—"

Both men whirled as a man screamed and staggered back from the bar, clutching the stumps of his fingers to his chest. Miko brandished a bloody knife in a gesture befitting an elementary school teacher admonishing a naughty pupil. Jimmy waved a hand at the scene and raised an eyebrow.

Corky sighed in disgust. "Fine. Take him...."

"Thanks—"

"If you can convince him to go."

"Damn it!" Jimmy said. He looked over at the lithe islander, trying to gauge the best way to go about things. Khuna was a mystery to Dolan. He was by turns touchy and jovial, with a mercurial temper that was backed up by a shark-tooth studded *koa* wood club and a Winchester Repeating Rifle.

Khuna had killed men for looking at him wrong, and there were rumors—which Corky thought were good for business—that he was still on the skull-road, taking heads in weekend raids to other islands in the chain.

Jimmy wasn't sure whether there were any truth to the rumors, but he'd seen the detritus of a Khuna rampage once or twice, and he wasn't eager to be in the middle of another. He sidled towards Khuna carefully. "Hey—ah—Khuna?"

"Hnh?" Khuna said, not looking up from his whittling.

"What do you know about Ghora?"

The whittling stopped. Khuna looked up and jammed his knife into the bar. "No," he said.

"No, as in you don't know anything?"

"No, as in I am not going," Khuna grunted.

"Why?"

Khuna looked at him, running his thumb along the top of the bone he'd been whittling. He said nothing. Jimmy threw up his hands. "Come on! I'll pay you."

"No amount of money is worth going to that island," Khuna said, tapping Jimmy's nose with the bone.

Jimmy named a figure. Khuna blinked, then: "Double it."

"What?"

Khuna pulled his knife free and prepared to go back to whittling. Jimmy made a placating gesture. "Fine. Double. Happy?"

"No."

"But you're coming?"

"Not if you keep asking," Khuna said. "When?"

"Tomorrow?"

Khuna looked at him. Jimmy cocked his head. "What? You have something better to do?"

"Always." Khuna blew air out through his nostrils. "Tomorrow. Meet you at the *Lucy Goosey*."

Jimmy grinned and slapped Khuna on the arm. The point of the latter's knife skittered across the bone. He looked at Jimmy's hand, then at Jimmy.

Dolan took the hint and backed off.

"Is he going?" Corky said, as Jimmy headed for the door.

"Yep." Jimmy grinned at Corky's expression of disapproval and slid into the night. The storm was winding down, having spent most of its fury. It was still drizzling though, and he put on his jacket, flipping up the collar.

Jimmy moved back towards the house/office he rented on the docks. He'd moved to Motugra a few years previous after getting trapped on the island by a storm just like the one that had just passed. He still ran cargo, but Motugra made a more effective base of operations. More profitable, too. There were any number of smuggling routes and shady enterprises scattered through the Motugra chain and on the coasts, and Jimmy always had an eye out for the main chance.

Behind him, feet splashed through the muddy streets. Jimmy heard them, but didn't turn. There were a lot of people out and about at night on the island. Not just townies, but native islanders and new arrivals. No reason to think anyone was following him. His hand found the pistol in his coat pocket regardless.

There was a hiss from the alleyway to his right. Jimmy stopped, then cursed himself for doing exactly what they'd wanted him to do. He juked to the side, pulling the Colt as he twisted around.

The *koa* club split the air as it curved through the space his head had been occupying only seconds previous. A second tooth-covered war club punched towards his face, and he rolled desperately, hitting the street in a splash of muddy water, his .45 belching.

Bare feet caught him in the belly and he curled instinctively as pain flared through his kidney. He snapped out a hand, grabbing an ankle and yanked with all of his strength, pulling his opponent off of his feet.

As the first man fell, the second chopped at Jimmy, forcing him to roll across the street. The man followed, making a high-pitched chitter of sound as he came. Jimmy cocked his hip, sweeping out his legs and catching the second man on the shins and sending him sprawling.

Dolan scrambled to his feet. The first attacker was back up as well, and Jimmy realized with a start that his face was hidden behind a wooden mask. In fact, both of them were wearing the things. They wore rag-bin trousers and had sharply angled tattoos scrawled across their brown flesh.

Another *koa* club cut through the distance between Jimmy and his opponents as the first man went on the attack again, chittering. It slapped into his chest, throwing him backwards in a spray of mud. Jimmy bounced up, the Colt bucking, and his second opponent gave a strangled shriek and flopped forward.

Breathing heavily, Jimmy turned. Khuna gave a lazy salute and moved past him to retrieve his sword from the dead man's chest.

"Were you following me?" Jimmy said, holstering his pistol.

"Saw them follow you out of the Monkey." Khuna grinned. "And if I hadn't, you'd be dead."

"Don't sound so blasted cheerful about it," Jimmy said, sinking to his haunches beside one of the dead men. He looked at the mask for a moment, then peeled it away from its owner's face. Khuna spat something in his native tongue.

"Looks like a damn bat," Jimmy said, eyeing the mask. He slapped it against his thigh and stood. "You ever seen tattoos like that?"

"Yes." Khuna didn't elaborate. Jimmy looked at him, then back at the bodies. They were Motugrans, that much he knew. But never any type he'd seen before.

Jimmy sighed. "Fine. Help me roll them into an alley."

"Why bother?" Khuna said, grabbing a pair of ankles.

Jimmy did likewise. "This town may not got laws against murder, but I'll be damned if I'm going to do another stretch in the Oven for littering," Jimmy said, referring to the island's main repository of law-breakers.

"I told you at the time that you shouldn't have left that car there," Khuna said.

"It was on fire," Jimmy said.

"That's no excuse."

"Funny, that's what the judge said."

"It hurts the tourist trade," Khuna said. Jimmy eyed him, then shook his head. They left the bodies in an out of the way spot, wedging them in among the rest of the detritus.

"Think there are any more of them out there?" Jimmy said when they had finished.

Khuna shrugged. "Probably."

"You say that like you know who they are. Were." Jimmy gestured. "Spill it."

"They're the reason we shouldn't be going to Ghora," Khuna said after a moment. "Eyes open." He used two fingers to indicate his eyes, and Jimmy's own. Then, he turned and headed back in the direction of the Monkey, leaving Jimmy staring after him.

"Thanks," Jimmy called out, then he continued on to his office. Still jittery with adrenaline, he checked behind doors and around corners with his hand inside his jacket, ready to draw down. Satisfied that no one intended to murder him, he tossed the mask on the steel desk that occupied one corner of the office, and sat down in a creaky wingback. He swung his feet up on the desk and watched the moonlight through the half-painted windows, thinking sour thoughts.

He looked at the mask. Khuna said they'd followed him, but he was pretty sure they'd followed someone else first. A certain sassy someone, with Swedish eyes and Sooner state hips. The question was, why? And why come after him?

Suspicion came naturally to someone in Jimmy's line of work. Had he champed down on a line of bait without realizing it? Or was Ms. Orne trailing sharks unawares? If he had to bet, it would have been on the latter.

But who were they? Frowning, he tapped the mask with a finger. "Hell, let's just ask her, then," he said out loud. Satisfied, he tipped his hat down over his face and leaned back. In moments, he was snoring. But his hand remained on his pistol.

Jimmy's dreams were worse than usual, and he woke early, heart hammering as if he'd been pursued over rough ground by something hungry. Cleaning out his mouth and mind with a shot of whiskey, he left the office and began to prepare for the day's flight.

An hour later, as he was double-checking the engines, a polite cough let him know that his passengers had arrived.

Sonia Orne looked up at him as he swung down off the wing and dropped to the dock. Behind her, a bevy of academics bobbed nervously. "Mr. Dolan? I hope we're not too early," Orne said.

"Bang on the dot, actually," Jimmy said, grinning. He cleaned his hands on a rag and stuffed it into his back pocket. "Is this everyone?"

They were a motley lot, all sunburns and khaki. All of them,—one woman and three men—looked like Orne-experienced field academics. The clothes were functional, and they were traveling light. Two of the men carried pistols on their belts, and Orne had a bolt-action rifle slung across her shoulder.

"Mr. Dolan, may I introduce Professor Francis Morgan," Orne began, gesturing to one of the men. Middle-aged, but athletic looking, Morgan shook Jimmy's hand without hesitation and without speaking. Orne continued, "Professor Warren Rice." A stocky, iron-gray man stepped forward, clapping Jimmy's hand in both of his.

"Damn fine to meet you. Damn fine," Rice said. Like Morgan, he was armed.

"And this is John Lapham," Orne said, indicating the youngest man, who was admiring the plane.

"Grumman Goose?" he said, nodding to Jimmy.

"Yep."

"What does she pull?"

"One hundred seventy-five knots, if the load is right," Jimmy said proudly. He reached up and slapped the wing. Orne shook her head, bemused by Dolan's enthusiasm, and gestured to the remaining member of the group. "Samantha Freeborn."

Jimmy blinked. "Like the guy we're looking for?"

"He's my husband, actually. Or at least he was when he left," Freeborn said. She was a lithe woman, slimmer than Orne, and darker, with a Boston Brahmin look. Blue blood pumped in her veins and tinted her accent. "Thank you, Mr. Dolan, for doing this...."

"Call me Jimmy," Jimmy said, his grin widening. The only thing better than a pretty woman was a pretty woman with money, and Jimmy had a suspicion that Samantha Freeborn was practically crawling under the weight of her bank account. "Besides, I'm getting paid well for my time."

Freeborn smiled. "And you can call me Sam. When Sonia told me your price, I thought she'd been duped. But here you are."

"I would never take advantage of a woman," Jimmy said, placing a hand over his heart.

Sam chuckled huskily. "Not unless she asked you to, right?"

"Knife to the heart, Sam," Jimmy said. "You'll get your money's worth, never fear. We'll find your husband."

"I have my doubts about that, come what may," Sam said bluntly.

Jimmy blinked. He caught sight of Orne out of the corner of his eye, and noticed she was glaring. His grin slipped into a smirk. He clapped his hands together. "We'll see. Hope springs eternal." He turned to the group. "The only one we're waiting on now is our trusty native guide."

"Been here for five minutes," Khuna said, from atop the wing. Everyone turned, and an oath spilled from Professor Rice's lips. The older man clawed for his pistol, but Jimmy latched onto his wrist with an iron grip.

"Whoa there! Khuna, you got to stop sneaking up on people," Jimmy said.

"Not my fault you didn't hear me," Khuna said, slipping to the dock. His club was sheathed across his back, and he carried a Winchester loosely in one brown fist. He'd replaced his decorative bandolier with a more functional one, heavy with cartridges. A British Webley rode low under his arm, in a shark-skin holster. "We ready?"

"Soon as we get their stuff aboard," Jimmy said, looking at the group. "May I present Khuna, your guide for this trip."

"I saw him at the bar last night!" Orne protested.

Jimmy made a placating gesture. "He occasionally moonlights as a bouncer, but I assure you that he's as experienced and trustworthy as they come!"

"Doubtful," Morgan said, uttering his first word of the day. "Taken many heads lately?"

"Only from people who annoy me." Khuna glanced at him, then looked at Jimmy.

"Yeah, yeah." Jimmy shrugged. "We're all friends here, right? Great."

As the group loaded their equipment into the plane, Jimmy pulled Orne aside. "I thought you said that university of yours was funding this trip?"

"When did I say that?" Orne said, innocently.

Jimmy snorted. "Don't play innocent. What's the deal?"

"The deal is just what I said it was...finding Tyler—I mean, Professor Freeborn."

"Yeah? Great. Got any ideas about this?" Jimmy said, retrieving the strange mask from where it lay with his tools in his rucksack.

Orne went quiet as she held the thing. Jimmy shifted impatiently. "Well?"

"Professor Freeborn had one of these. From an earlier expedition to this area," she said, slowly. "It's a ceremonial mask...from Ghora." She looked at him with suspicion. "Where did you get this?"

"It fell into my lap," Jimmy said. "Is it valuable?"

"To the right people, yes. It's a stylized representation of something

Professor Freeborn called 'Gorogoro', I think." Orne turned the mask over and traced the interior curve. "This is *blood!*"

"How about that?" Jimmy said nonchalantly, as he plucked the mask out of her grip. "Time to go, lady."

"But where did you—"

"Daylight is burning, and time is money. My time, your money. Everybody on the plane!" Jimmy bellowed the latter and gestured. The academics piled in, and Jimmy and Khuna climbed into the pilot's compartment.

Engines purring with a steady rumble, the Grumman Goose cut through the water and, in minutes, was swooping upwards with barely a tremor to mark the air's resistance. Jimmy caressed the controls gently, leveling the plane off and pointing its nose in the direction of Ghora.

After a moment, he turned slightly and glanced back at his passengers. "We've got about an hour before we reach the island, so sit back and relax, folks."

"Have you flown this route before, Jimmy?" Sam said, leaning forward.

"Once. Usually, the more aeronautically-minded among our lovely community steer clear of Ghora. Water-rats as well. Not a good spot to get engine failure, if you get my drift."

"Tyler seemed to think the natives were rather civilized," Rice said. "Moreso than the average run of Motugran...no offense to our guide."

Khuna grunted.

Jimmy shook his head. "Doc, there's a good reason Ghora is called 'The Island That Eats Men' by the locals."

"Head-hunters?" Morgan said.

Khuna chuckled.

"Nope. Khuna is a head-hunter. Or was, before he got a real job." Jimmy grinned at his passengers. "The Ghora are just plain cannibals."

"Oh, my," Sam said, frowning. "That doesn't sound at all like the idyllic vacation spot Tyler made it out to be in his letters."

"That'd be why Rice and Morgan brought guns," Lapham said, seated in the back of the plane. The young man was semi-sprawled out beside Orne, his head tilted back. "I'd have brought one too, if I could hit the broadside of a barn."

"More likely, you'd hit one of us," Orne said. "Besides, I'm sure we won't need them."

"Then why did you bring that rifle, hmmm?" Freeborn said lazily. Orne flushed.

"Food, of course. There are any number of edible species on these

Orne turned the mask over and traced the interior curve. "This is *blood!*"

islands-pigs, monkeys, fowl...."

"Hate to disappoint you, babe, but Ghora is renowned for being a bad place to safari. Unless it got there on a ship-wreck, it ain't there."

"Then what do the natives eat?" Orne said, eyebrow quirked.

Jimmy laughed. "I thought I made that clear before. They eat each other."

"Rats," Khuna said.

"Rats?" Sam said.

Khuna glanced over his shoulder. "Lots of rats."

"Rat's good, with the right sauce," Jimmy added.

Surprisingly, Morgan nodded. "Depends on the species, but hot sauce will do for most."

"Francis!" Rice sounded shocked.

Morgan shrugged. "One man's vermin is another man's delicacy."

Jimmy chuckled. He was beginning to warm to the taciturn professor, despite his initial misgivings. "So, Sonia mentioned something about Freeborn studying the local nutjobs...."

"The religious practices of the Ghoral natives are fascinating," Orne said. "At least I thought so."

Lapham snorted. "You and Freeborn were the only two."

"Be fair, Johnny, me lad, you'd have been more open to the idea if Tyler had picked you to accompany him to Ghora, instead of Sonia," Rice said.

"You were supposed to go with him?" Jimmy said, surprised. Orne shifted uncomfortably.

"Unfortunately, she had to decline," Sam said softly. "Isn't that right, Sonia?"

"Yes," Orne said, between gritted teeth.

Jimmy blinked. "Huh. Well." He glanced at Khuna, who gazed steadily out at the clouds. An uncomfortable silence descended for the longest ten minutes of Jimmy's life, until Rice cleared his throat.

"Been in Motugra long, Mr. Dolan?" he said.

"Call me Jimmy. But yeah, a few years. Why do you ask?"

"Are the criminals always so bold, or is that a recent occurrence?" Rice said, half-chuckling.

"Criminals?" Jimmy asked.

"Last night. Someone tried to get into our room at the establishment we were staying at. Bugger had the door half open before Morgan noticed."

"When he heard me cock my pistol, he beat feet," Morgan said.

"Hunh. Someone tried to get into my room, too," Lapham said. "I thought I saw someone looking in my window." He glanced at Orne. "What about you, Sonia?"

Orne looked away. "No. Nothing."

Jimmy looked at Khuna, who shook his head slightly. Jimmy sniffed, and feigned ignorance. "Never heard of that, but we've got a rough element, that I cannot deny."

"You might, but not for much longer. I heard that the Japanese are making noises about territorial possession," Rice said.

"That's not news," Jimmy said, leaning forward to tap a dial on his control panel. "The Japanese, the French, the British, everybody and their brother thinks they own these islands. Of course, owning and wanting are two entirely different things." A shadow drifted across the nose of the plane, and he jerked his head up. Had it been a bird?

"Meaning?"

"Not a good bargain," Khuna said, answering before Jimmy could. "We're still here."

"I doubt the Japanese are worried overmuch," Rice said. "No offense."

Khuna grunted.

Jimmy looked at him. "What?"

"I didn't mean to imply—" Rice began, but Jimmy waved him to silence.

Khuna slapped the window. "Something is—"

The plane shrieked and shuddered. Jimmy fought the stick, trying to hold the Goose steady. Smoke billowed off of one wing. Khuna began to curse in his own tongue, as Sam screamed and the others yelled questions or imprecations. Jimmy didn't waste time telling them to shut up. The dials wobbled crazily, and he knew an engine had failed and the plane had been knocked off course.

The burning wing dipped, and Jimmy's hands and wrists ached as he made war on gravity. A mass of black and brown and green was rapidly filling the windscreen. "Everyone hold on! We're going to have a bit of a bump!"

More questions, but Jimmy ducked his head and aimed the Goose towards the blue patch just south of the green. Better the water than the trees. If he could just get her steady....

The landing wasn't the smoothest he had ever managed, but neither was it the worst. He cut the engine as the plane slewed across the water of the small lagoon, slowing as it approached the beach on its belly and pontoons. Jimmy gave a low whistle as the props—rather, the remaining prop—slowed and finally stopped.

"Well, that was exhilarating," Sam said, after a stretch of silence.

"Let's not do it again, though," Orne said. "What in the hell happened, Mr. Dolan?"

"Something hit us," Khuna said, opening his door and dropping into the green-blue water.

"Did it?" Rice said.

Jimmy unbuckled his safety harness and shrugged. "Possibly. Bird, maybe. Or it could have been something lodged in there from the last flight. Either way, everybody out."

"Can you fix it?" Lapham said, hauling open the door at the back.

"Yeah. No," Jimmy said. "Maybe if I had magic powers." He hauled himself out of his seat and up onto the top of the plane. He moved towards the opposite wing, covering his face with his hand as smoke coiled towards him. Crouched near the engine, he said, "Somebody get me the damn fire extinguisher!"

"Just throw water on it," Orne said.

"Salt water will corrode what's left of this engine, so I'm thinking no," Jimmy said. Lapham scrambled half-way up onto the plane, thrusting the extinguisher towards Jimmy. The latter grabbed it and sprayed foam liberally across the engine, damping the flames.

He sighed disgustedly as he looked at the engine. "We'll need to tow her back."

"Does that mean we won't be making it to Ghora?" Orne said, shading her eyes and looking at the wall of trees that rose up off of the beach.

Jimmy snorted. "Nope. Just means we won't be flying out."

"We're here?" She looked around, eyes wide.

"Yep." Jimmy hopped off of the wing into the water. The plane had taxied to a stop just on the edge of the beach, and water lapped at the landing gear. Jimmy moved around towards the back and began to help the others unload their gear. "Not exactly where I'd planned to set down, but close enough."

Khuna loped back towards the group. "Crater is north of us. We'll have to go through the jungle," he said grimly.

"Yeah. Figures," Jimmy said, stepping back and glancing at the damaged wing. Something hung from the wreckage and he reached out to touch it. Khuna grabbed his wrist.

"Don't," the Motugran said.

"What? Why?"

Khuna gestured with his rifle. Jimmy turned, then swore. "Crap in a sack!"

"What?" Rice said. He and the others came over.

"Is that…blood?" Sam said, nose wrinkling.

"Astounding," Lapham said, leaning close to the runny spray that coated the underside of the wing and the side of the plane.

"I thought it was just oil," Jimmy said. "So what does that make this?" He indicated the chunk of matter dangling from the engine. It was long and leathery and a strong smell emanated from it. Like sulfur and ammonia and blood.

"What exactly hit us?" Morgan said, glancing at Khuna.

Khuna spat. "Need to get moving."

"Yeah." Jimmy shook himself. "Give me a minute." He climbed back into the pilot's compartment and flicked a few switches, bringing his radio to life. Switching frequencies, he found the right one and squeezed the call button. "Hey, anyone got their ears open? Nicky?"

There was the sound of fumbling, then a squawk of static, and a sleep-addled voice said, "Yeah? Jimmy?"

"Nick, got a problem."

"So what's new?" Nick Fortune grunted. The captain of a low-riding rumrunner, Fortune made his living on the fringes just like Jimmy. He plied the waters, and Jimmy the skies, but they moved in the same circles, namely those few regular patrons of the Hanging Monkey. "What do you want this time, Dolan?"

"Still got that tow-line you borrowed from Jenkins? The one he doesn't know you borrowed?"

"Yeah," Fortune said slowly.

"I need you to tow my baby. I had an engine failure and had to put down near Ghora."

"Near Ghora?" Fortune said suspiciously.

"Fine. On Ghora. Southern lagoon, near as I can figure. I need a ride out."

"When?"

"Two days?"

"Long time to be on Ghora, Jimmy," Fortune said.

"Is that concern I hear in your voice, Nicky?" Jimmy said, grinning.

There was a muffled snort. "You still owe me for the last time I bailed you out, Dolan."

"Well, add this to my tab then. Forty-eight hours. I'll be on the beach." Jimmy rattled off the latitude and longitude. "Got that?"

"Fine. Forty-eight hours. Don't make me wait, Dolan. I do have better things to do than ferry you back and forth."

"Don't we all. You're a brick, Nicky."

"I hate you," Fortune said.

Jimmy laughed and switched off the radio. He hopped out of the plane and looked at the others. "That's our ride back taken care of. Grab your gear, everyone. No sense wasting any more time." He checked his Colt, then scooped a bolt-action rifle out from the luggage compartment. Slinging it over his shoulder, he followed Khuna up the beach, the others trailing behind. "Everyone stay close. Don't get separated. Don't wander off."

Lapham, just behind Jimmy, swiftly assembled a camera as he walked. Jimmy looked at him and shook his head. He glanced at Orne. "Freeborn's camp was near the crater, right?"

"According to his letters, yes," Sam interjected, before Orne could reply. The younger woman glared at her, but nodded in assent.

"He said he was on the north slope," Orne added. "How long do you think it will take us to reach it?"

"Depends on how much trouble we run into along the way," Jimmy said. He looked around, shading his eyes with his hand. The Ghoral Crater rose dimly out of the tree-line, shrouded in dense clouds of fog. It squatted, black and toad-like, in the center of the island, and it seemed to radiate impersonal hostility. Jimmy felt a chill slither down his spine and he whistled softly.

Orne followed his gaze. "Volcanic gases. Or so Professor Freeborn's letters said. The crater still emits them, every so often."

"Don't tell me that." Jimmy grimaced and scraped his knuckles across his cheek. "Dangerous?"

"Depends on how much you breathe in, one assumes," Orne said, smiling slightly at his discomfort. "You could stay with the plane, Mr. Dolan."

"And let the lot of you go tramping off? No way, lady. You still owe me the rest of my money." Jimmy looked up at the sky. "We're burning daylight. Let's move."

In a rough single-file line, they moved into the jungle, Khuna in the lead. The islander was as tense as Jimmy had ever seen, every wiry muscle on his frame standing out. It wasn't fear, exactly, but Khuna wasn't saying something. Then, Khuna never said much.

For his own part, Jimmy felt the weight of the wooden mask in his pack. Orne said it was from Ghora…so how had it gotten to Motugra? Had his attackers been natives? And if so, why had they been following Orne?

The trees were thin on the beach, bunching up closer and closer as the sand gave way to scrub vines and grass. Fat trunks and spear-blade leaves became taller, looming trees, that formed a green ceiling, blocking out all but a drizzle of sunlight. Roots as thick as a man's arm curled across the forest floor, creating layer after layer of hidey-holes and stumbling points.

It was quiet as well; not even a whisper of birdsong. That was the worst thing, to Jimmy's mind. Sweat rolled down his face, cutting trails in the grime left by the smoke and exertion.

By the third hour, they were puffing. Rice sounded like a beached whale, and he was covered in a sheen of perspiration. Sam was looking shaky, obviously unused to a pace like Khuna's. Lapham, lugging his camera, was putting on a brave face, but it was slipping steadily.

Orne, in contrast, looked perkier than before, as if the climate and rough going agreed with her. Or maybe she was just looking forward to seeing Professor Freeborn again. Jimmy smiled at the thought. Definitely something going on there.

Morgan didn't seem too bothered by either the pace or the heat, unlike Rice. The quiet professor moved determinedly, bringing up the rear, his eyes sweeping the jungle with wary intensity.

Jimmy, for his part, felt more at home with his butt in a seat than his boots on the ground. Still, he'd made worse hikes.

Khuna stopped and raised a hand sometime later. He looked at Jimmy. "I'll go ahead. Take a look. Make sure the trail is clear."

"You heard the man," Jimmy said, dropping onto his haunches, his back against a tree. Khuna vanished into the trees without a backward glance.

Rice fell onto his back, breathing heavily. Lapham took a picture of the dark canopy overhead. Sam sat near Jimmy. "Got a light?" she said, leaning forward. Jimmy grinned and popped his lighter to life.

Puffing contentedly, Sam leaned back and looked around the clearing where Khuna had left them. "I saw something last night as well, you know," she said softly.

"Oh?" Jimmy lit a cigarette for himself.

"Guy in a mask." She hesitated. "I hope it was a mask. Staring right through the window at me, bold as blazes."

"Peeping Tom," Jimmy said, though without conviction.

"I don't think so," Sam said, leaning towards him. "Tell you something else...."

"Yeah?"

"I don't think my husband wants to be found."

Jimmy blinked. "Hunh." He sucked on his cigarette for a moment, considering. Then, "You said he had a mask?"

"Yeah. Why?"

"Got something I want to show you," he said, wrestling his pack off and opening it up. His fingers closed on the mask, but before he could pull it out, Lapham screamed.

Jimmy shot to his feet as the younger man stumbled, something dark wrapped around his head. Morgan reached him first and pulled the thing—whatever it was—off.

"God Almighty, it's a rat!" Rice said, rolling to his feet with a wheeze.

"Dead rat," Morgan said, shooting the creature as it bounded to its feet, hairless tail lashing.

Sam shot to her feet with a shriek and pointed. "More of them!"

Jimmy turned and saw more rats scrambling through the entwined roots of the trees. They didn't seem to be heading anywhere in particular. He snatched up his pack, shaking off a rat that clung to it. "Ignore 'em," he said, moving to Sam's side. "Ignore them! They're just swarming." He took her shoulders and pulled her into an embrace as the rats moved through the clearing. Morgan didn't put his gun away, but he didn't fire again.

Lapham was shaking. He clutched his camera to him and blew out a noisy breath. His face was covered in scratches. Orne grabbed his chin and tilted his face, examining him. "We need to get some antiseptic on those bites. Who knows what those things were carrying."

"Jesus," Sam whispered under her breath. Jimmy coughed and stepped back from her, looking around.

"You can say that again. I wonder what that was about," he said. He found his eyes drawn once more to the crater, where it jutted from the greenery. It seemed even more imposing the closer they got to it. Flying shapes drifted lazily through the dark clouds of gas that hung close to the slopes. Jimmy squinted but couldn't make them out.

"Hunh," he said.

Sam looked at him. "What?"

"Nothing. Must be some birds here after all," Jimmy said. "That's weird."

A lump of rat bodies, tied together by the tails, dropped into the clearing. Khuna shimmied down one of the wide trees and dropped lightly onto the roots.

"Something is hunting," he said. He glanced at Morgan and frowned. "Shouldn't have fired that pistol, though."

"The hell he shouldn't have! I almost lost my face!" Lapham sputtered as Orne tended to him.

"Did you bring enough for everyone?" Jimmy said, gesturing to the dead rats.

"Get your own," Khuna said. He slung the rats over his shoulder and looked around. "We can go. The way is clear."

"Clear of what?" Morgan said, suspiciously.

"Everything. Anything," Khuna said.

Despite a muttered protest from Rice, the group set off again, moving slowly. Occasionally, someone would spot a rat scrambling through the roots or across a branch, but never any more than that.

Jimmy could feel their eyes, however. He could tell the creatures were watching them with the wary intensity of animals which were not afraid, but merely curious. He tried to ignore it, but he found his fingers playing a nervous pitter-pat on the butt of his Colt regardless.

They hit the juju sticks fifteen minutes later. It probably wasn't the proper term, but Jimmy wasn't in the mood to ask.

The wooden sticks littered the ground, stabbed between roots and jutting at odd angles. Strips of leather had been used to lash skulls and other assorted bones to the sticks. Rice and Morgan both expressed something Jimmy assumed was professional interest, the former crouching close to one of the sticks, getting to eye-level with a yellowed skull.

Khuna seemed ill at ease, and Jimmy couldn't blame him. The Motugran shifted impatiently as the group came to a dead stop. Lapham unlimbered his camera, and the flashbulb was soon popping.

"Don't touch anything," Khuna said. "We should keep moving," he continued, looking at Jimmy.

"Agreed. Plenty of time to look at dead things later," Jimmy said.

"Nominally, this is a research trip," Lapham said, taking another picture. "May as well do some actual research."

"Rescue first, research after," Jimmy said, snapping his fingers. "Wrap it up."

Sam stood closer to Jimmy, something he couldn't bring himself to mind. "It's horrible," she said.

"No. It's cultural," Orne snorted. "They're just territorial markers. Nothing to be afraid of." The Midwesterner jabbed one of the skulls with the barrel of her rifle. Khuna spun, reaching out, but too late.

There was the sound of snapping vines and then the creak of wood. Jimmy reacted without thought, tackling Orne to the ground as the sharpened stakes dropped from the trees and imbedded themselves in the ground where she'd been standing.

"He said not to touch anything!" Jimmy snarled, rising to his feet, pistol out. Khuna had his rifle ready and both men scanned the surrounding forest. "Damn. Khuna?"

"We need to move. Now."

Jimmy grabbed Orne's arm and jerked her to her feet. "Go."

"What was that?" Orne said as he pushed her along. "Was that a booby-trap?"

"It's like a damn Republic serial," Morgan said, casting wary glances at the trees. "Tyler must have been crazy to come here—"

"He wasn't crazy!" Orne snapped, turning. "And he's a better man than you!"

"Enough!" Sam snapped, forcing herself between them. Morgan stepped back as he caught sight of the look on her face. Orne hesitated and Sam grabbed her arm. "Tyler doesn't need you to defend him," she said. "Not anymore."

"Someone has to!" Orne snarled, jerking her arm free. "If I'd been here with him, maybe he wouldn't have disappeared."

"Or maybe you both would have," Rice interjected, gently pulling Orne away from the other woman. "We need to keep moving, I think. Just like our guides have suggested." Rice looked at Jimmy, who nodded.

"We need to find someplace to make camp. Someplace defensible, if it comes to that."

"You think it will?" Lapham said, looking nervous.

"No. But better safe than sorry, right?" Jimmy said, attempting a smile. No one looked like they were buying it.

The forest seemed to close around them, advancing with every blink of the eyes or turn of the head. The trees curled and slumped like arthritic giants, and the darkness grew as the sun dropped below the rim of the crater overhead.

Jimmy trotted ahead of the group. Khuna slowed so that the two men could move side-by-side. "What's the skinny?" Jimmy said quietly.

"We're in someone's territory," Khuna grunted. "And they're out there, right now."

"Watching us?"

"Waiting," Khuna said harshly.

"For what?"

Khuna shrugged and shook his head. "Something bad."

"You're a born pessimist, ain'tcha?" Jimmy said. "I saw some birds."

"There aren't any birds on the island."

"Nonetheless, I saw them."

"*Gorogoro*," Khuna muttered.

Jimmy looked at him. "That's the second time I've heard that word. What is it?"

"Not a bird," Khuna said.

"Orne said it was a god."

"Still not a bird."

Jimmy threw up his hands. "Fine. Not a bird. Going to answer my question?"

"It's just a story," Khuna said, his head swiveling, as if he were trying to see everything at once. "*Gorogoro* comes in the night and snatches bad children. Or loose women. Or drunken men. Anyone disagreeable."

"The boogeyman?" Jimmy touched his pack, feeling for the mask. "So those guys last night were from these parts, huh?"

"Yes."

"Means they probably know we're coming, right?"

"Yes," Khuna said again.

Jimmy made a sound of disgust. "Wonderful. You ever met them before?"

"Once or twice. Bad people," Khuna said. "Nice skulls, though."

"Oh, well, that makes it all right." Jimmy shook his head, then rubbed sweat out of his eyes. "Anything else I should know?"

"They don't care for visitors."

"Really? Ducky. Why are we here, then?" Jimmy said in exasperation.

Khuna rubbed his fingers together. "Money."

"Right. Right. Damn," Jimmy said, looking at the darkening sky. "I did not think this through."

They made camp in a bower as night descended. The lattice of interlocking tree branches overhead provided a protective canopy as the rain started up. It rattled the wide leaves and punched ripples into the surfaces of the tents. Jimmy and Morgan wrestled a canvas stand up over the fire, protecting it from the rain, as Rice set to butchering the rats Khuna had captured.

Khuna himself climbed up into one of the trees, his Winchester wrapped in oilcloth. Jimmy watched him disappear, and unsnapped the fold on his holster. Just in case. If Khuna said someone was watching them, then someone was watching them.

If only the plane hadn't messed up, they could have landed closer to the crater, avoiding the jungle entirely. Jimmy peered through the rain, wondering again what it was they'd hit. It had to have been something big to have torn up the engine that badly.

"Going to answer my question?"

Instinctively, he looked up at the sky, trying to pierce the starless gloom. What the hell was flying around up there?

"Surprisingly, it smells good," Sam said, interrupting Jimmy's thoughts, as she poured a tin of beans into a small iron pan that someone had placed over the fire. She stirred them as Rice dumped chunks of sliced rat into the nascent stew.

"My deft touch, of course," Rice said, grinning. "I carry a spice grinder wherever I go."

"It's true," Morgan said. "We had to go back for it in Australia, despite being chased by angry locals."

"Not my fault those colonial heathens didn't appreciate the subtle tang of coriander and cumin," Rice said, looking hurt.

Morgan laughed. "I think it was the chili pepper you topped things off with that did it."

Lapham sat fiddling with his camera. Jimmy crouched near him. "Good shots?" he said.

"Plenty. Photography is a bit of a hobby of mine." Lapham patted the camera. "Thought about going into journalism, actually."

"But?" Jimmy said, interested despite himself.

"Things never seem to work out for me," Lapham said, smiling self-deprecatingly. He gestured towards Orne. "For instance, I was Freeborn's assistant before Sonia got to Miskatonic."

"I take it there was something going on there," Jimmy said, waggling his fingers at Sam, who smiled at him from her spot by the cooking fire. Lapham caught the gesture and made a sound that might have been a chuckle.

"Several somethings."

"Cause trouble?"

"More than once." Lapham raised his camera and took a shot of the group around the fire. "I figure Freeborn was glad to get away from it all. If I was him, I'd have wanted to disappear, too." He lowered his camera. "Hey, you hear something?"

Jimmy glanced over his shoulder, letting his eyes sweep the darkness. Distant pinpricks of light reached his eyes, like fires billowing to life on the slopes of the crater. Freeborn's natives? Or worse, Khuna's boogeyman?

"Hunh." Jimmy stood, reaching for his rifle.

"You hear it too, right? Sounds like...drums?" Lapham said, getting to his feet.

"No," Jimmy said. "Ah, hell...."

Claws scraped over bark and then the rats spilled out of the darkness, a wave of furry, moving bodies that slammed into his legs like squirming torpedoes. He fell and was bowled under, his rifle skidding away. They bit and clawed at him as they trampled over him. He heard the others yelling, and heard Morgan's pistol snap.

Jimmy slapped a rat off his chest and scrambled to his feet, using a tree for support. The rats kept coming, hundreds, thousands. In the darkness, Jimmy thought he saw figures moving. The rats knocked over the stew, dousing the cooking fire in a spray of blue flame and steam.

Something crashed down through the trees with a shriek like metal tearing. A woman screamed, whether Orne or Sam, Jimmy couldn't say as he whirled, dragging his pistol free of its holster.

A smell invaded the bower, like rotten eggs and ammonia. Something hissed like a bellows. Jimmy saw a vague bulk flop towards him, far too big to be a man.

Someone—Lapham, Jimmy thought—suddenly screamed. Jimmy smelled blood and took a chance, firing his Colt. In the strobe burst of the gun going off, he saw a nightmare. And it saw him.

The thing's skull was sloped with a flared, spear-blade nose and blind, black eyes, topped by immense, black worm-veined ears that seemed to swivel and turn at every noise. But its mouth was the worst. The teeth were like six inch needles, slim and wicked looking, bared open in a silent shriek around a pale pink tongue.

All of this, Jimmy saw in brief, intermittent flashes as the creature spun and flopped towards him, hissing like a ruptured boiler.

A howling war-cry echoed suddenly, causing the thing to look away. Khuna fell from the trees, war-club swinging. The thing shrilled as the islander landed atop it. Jimmy charged forward, Colt barking. Something long and leathery struck him, sending him spinning. He hit the ground hard and rolled up against a tree. He heard the crack-snap of great wings and then the thing was lunging upwards, Khuna still clinging to its back!

Jimmy shot to his feet. "Damn it! Khuna!" He lunged, but his hands fell far short as the bulk of the beast heaved past the canopy of trees and was gone, disappearing into the vast darkness above.

"What was that? What the hell was that?" Rice shouted from somewhere in the darkness.

"*Gorogoro*," someone said.

Torches burst to life around the bower. Men in hideous wooden masks crouched or stood around the group. They carried shark-toothed club-swords and strangely curved spears. One or two held rifles, which they aimed at the group unwaveringly.

A spatter of words rattled from one of them. Orne replied, haltingly. She looked at the others.

"They want us to go with them."

"You speak their lingo?" Jimmy said.

"Somewhat. We need to go."

"What about John?" Sam said. Jimmy looked to where Lapham lay. The thing, the creature, *Gorogoro*, had apparently landed on him, mauling him in the process. Morgan squatted beside the contorted body. He looked at Jimmy and shook his head.

"Guess he was right. Things never worked out for him," Jimmy said heavily, picking up the broken camera. A native slapped it out of his hand. Jimmy turned and drove a fist into the man's belly, doubling him up. His knee rose, meeting the chin under the mask, and the Ghora toppled. Sword points pricked his flesh and he grudgingly raised his hands. One of the masked men jerked his pistol out of his grip, and the others were likewise similarly disarmed.

"I don't think they mean to hurt us," Orne said, handing her rifle over to one. "Freeborn," she said to the closest of them. "Ty-ler Free-born."

There was a ripple of something through their ranks. Masked faces traded looks. Then, Jimmy and the others were herded into the darkness.

From overhead came the caterwauling shrieks of what could only be the *Gorogoro*, and Jimmy shivered in sympathy for Khuna. The stocky warrior hadn't been a friend, exactly, but close enough. And he had saved Jimmy's life the previous night.

"What was that thing?" Sam murmured.

"Big and nasty," Jimmy said.

"Looked like a bat," Rice said.

"Whatever it was, I think something like it hit the plane," Jimmy said. "Our bad luck to be flying low in the clouds...."

A grunt from one of the Ghora put an end to any more conversation. The Ghora surrounded the group, the men carrying the torches holding them high so as to cast the maximum amount of light, despite the rain.

Jimmy watched them, cutting his eyes upward every so often. He thought again of the flying shapes he'd seen, and the hairs on the back of his neck prickled. Too, he thought of the stampeding rats. He looked at the torches carried by their captors and thought of the campfire going out.

They marched through most of the night, urged on whenever they began to slow. By the end, Morgan was supporting a wheezing Rice, and Jimmy had a steadying hand on Sam's hip. Orne moved faster than the others, almost eagerly.

As sunlight crawled up the sides of the crater, they left the trees and reached a rocky plateau that was lined with what might have once been the remains of a large wall. Shacks and lean-tos were crammed up against the stone, and the stink of cooking meat wafted through the makeshift streets.

People came out of the shacks and watched as the group was brought into the village. Children ran naked between the legs of their elders and women whispered fearfully. Jimmy noticed that a net of vines, leaves and shredded bark had been set up over most of the main drag, like a protective canopy. He also noted the plinths and broken columns that stuck out of the ground at odd points, and the ugly stains that marred those structures. He grimaced and spat, guessing what they were for.

"That stone there was shaped," Rice said, to no one in particular. "With tools."

"Freeborn said he'd found evidence of civilization," Morgan said, looking around, face grim. "Looks like he was right."

"And you didn't believe him," Orne said, victoriously. She glanced over her shoulder at them. "Neither of you!" She flung a hand out. "Look!"

Jimmy followed her gesture and saw square shapes clinging to the slope, all tumbledown and half-buried in rock and dirt, but still recognizable as having once been houses or buildings of some sort. Some even looked as if they were in the process of being dug out.

There were colored tiles scattered and chunks of carved stone in the dirt and piled up along the path. Jimmy turned and looked back. The forest of Ghora spread out behind and below him, and he could make out further ruins of pale stone here and there, just barely visible among the trees. Tendrils of smoke rose from among some of them, hinting at other groups.

"Wonder what happened," he said.

"It's obvious, isn't it?" Morgan said. He hiked a thumb over his shoulder at the Ghoral Crater, rising above them. "Volcano erupted, most likely. Like Pompeii."

"As intuitive as ever, Francis," someone said. Sam went pale as a man in a cloak made of some kind of dark leather stepped out of one of the shacks, his face hidden behind an ornate mask. Where the masks of the other men were crude affairs, this one was of almost museum quality, brightly painted and shiny.

"T-Tyler?" Rice stuttered.

"Warren. Still indulging in elevenses, I see," Tyler Freeborn said, removing his mask and smiling at the group. "Hello, Samantha. And, ah, Sonia as well. Is John here, too?"

"He's dead," Jimmy said. Freeborn looked at him.

"Ah. How unfortunate. I was looking forward to utilizing his skill with a camera." Freeborn was a mild looking man, burned bronze by a lifetime outdoors, and with the hard muscle of a man who'd been hard living for a long time.

"You knew we were coming," Morgan said.

Freeborn smiled. "I thought you might, yes." He looked at Jimmy. "Ah, the pilot?"

"Dolan. Jimmy Dolan. You can call me Mr. Dolan," Jimmy said, crossing his arms. Freeborn smiled again.

"Of course."

"So was it you who sent those guys after me," Jimmy said.

"Guys?" Orne said.

"Two of my best, in fact. I didn't want any outsiders involved in this expedition." Freeborn sniffed. "They were overzealous, I admit. I apologize most profusely. Hello, Sonia," he said, smiling benignly at his assistant. Orne looked at Samantha, then dove into Freeborn's arms.

"I thought you were dead," Orne said as Freeborn wrapped his arms around her.

"So did I. Care to explain, Tyler?" Sam said, face stiff. She rubbed her arms.

"Reports of my demise were greatly exaggerated. I'm impressed you came, dear," Freeborn said, pushing Sonia aside, "but not surprised."

"Shame. You know how I live to surprise you," Sam said sharply. Orne stiffened, but Freeborn chuckled.

He made a lazy gesture. "What does it matter now? You're here and things will proceed as they will, yes?"

"No. I don't know what you've gotten into here, Tyler but we're leaving," Morgan snapped. "I came out of respect for a colleague I thought was in trouble."

"As did I," Rice barked.

"No. You came to see whether I was right or not. Regardless, just as I hoped. Dear Sonia always excelled at guessing my needs," Freeborn said. Orne smiled. "Besides, I am in trouble, Francis." Freeborn clapped his hands and a number of women stepped forward, carrying baskets containing oddly shaped fruits, shredded leaves and cooked meats. "But we have plenty of time to discuss that. I'm sure you're starving and probably tired."

"I don't think—" Rice began. A war-club tapped his cheek and he cried out.

"I insist," Freeborn said. "Besides, when have you ever turned down a meal, Warren?"

They sat on the ground, eating in silence. The Ghora crouched, watching them, or eating themselves. Freeborn sat on his haunches with an easy grace. He chatted quietly with several of his men, their guttural tongue slipping easily out of his mouth. After a moment, he looked at Jimmy.

"I am sorry about your friend. My men tell me he died bravely, if that's any consolation."

"His name was Khuna," Jimmy said.

"Hmmm. Yes," Freeborn said. "The *Gorogoro* have doubtless consumed him by now. They are a rapacious species."

"Species? You mean there's more than one?" Morgan said.

"Of course," Freeborn said. "*Desmodus camazotz*, the prehistoric vampire bat."

"There's no such classification," Rice protested. "There's no such animal!"

"Really? Seemed pretty real to me," Jimmy said.

"They've been here for quite a while," Freeborn said. "Long enough to assume an evolutionary niche, at any rate." He chewed methodically on a chunk of cooked rat. "I came here following the stories. You recall the notes that came in as part of the Warren bequest a few years ago?" he continued, directing the last towards Morgan and Rice. "The Legrasse notebooks?"

"Vaguely," Rice said hesitantly.

"The black-winged ones," Morgan said, nodding.

"*Ahool. Olitiau. Kongamato. Guiafairo. Sasabonsam. Orang-Bati*," Freeborn said, rattling off syllables like machine-gun bullets. "*Gorogoro*."

"Excuse me for not being educated and all, but what?" Jimmy said.

Freeborn laughed. "Stories about giant bats abound throughout the world. From New Guinea to Java to Senegal to Indonesia, South America, North America and beyond. All the same thing."

"I thought you were an anthropologist, not one of them guys who study animals," Jimmy said.

Freeborn chuckled. "I am, I am. Folklore is my main area of interest. And the links between certain folk-stories is of particular fascination to me." He rubbed two fingers down the material of his cape. "For instance, the stories of great bats invariably intersect with those of lost civilizations."

He gestured to the village. "They worship them, you know. And fear them." He pointed up at the nets that blocked out the sky.

Jimmy snapped his fingers. "The fires!"

"Yes," Freeborn said. "The creatures don't like light. Damn near blinds them, in fact. I understand that you hit one earlier."

"Yeah," Jimmy said, wondering if Freeborn had had people on the beach, watching them. Had the Ghora been keeping pace with them all this time?

Freeborn nodded. "They were returning from the hunt. Sometimes they get caught in the daylight and go in the wrong direction, poor brutes."

"And the rat stampede?" Jimmy said, plucking a hunk of meat from one of the baskets and eyeing it. He watched a fat rat trundle across the open space, utterly unafraid of anything or anyone. "That's got something to do with them as well, don't it?"

"Oh, yes." Freeborn snapped an order and a spear flashed. The rat squealed as it was impaled and hoisted aloft. "The rats have co-existed with men here for as long as the *Gorogoro*. And both men and rats fear the 'terror-that-flies-by-night.' When the *Gorogoro* flies, the rats run."

"None of this explains why you wanted us here," Rice said. "Or how you came to be in charge of these people."

"Happy accident on the latter. They intended to sacrifice me to the *Gorogoro*…a barbaric little practice that I have, as yet, been unable to wean them off of." He motioned to the stained plinths. "The beasties have even come to expect it, if you can believe that!" Freeborn picked up his mask and stood. "Luckily, there are at least four other tribes on this island, none of which my friends here feel any affection for."

"But how did you come to be in charge?" Rice said.

"I'm getting to that, Warren. Don't jump ahead," Freeborn said. "The mask. This mask here." He lifted the mask to his face and placed it on his face. "It came via the Sanbourne Institute. They sent a relatively disastrous expedition to Motugra in 1921, looking into the unique ruins that dot the island chain. Just like those ruins out there…intriguing, no?"

"Get back to the point, Tyler," Morgan said.

"So impatient, Francis. Forgive me, but it's been a good long while since I've had any intelligent conversation." Freeborn sniffed and removed the mask. "The mask belonged to someone fairly high up the food chain, as it were, I believe. Their masks are merely crude copies of this one." He indicated the gathered tribesmen. "Luckily, I brought it with me. Equally luckily, I managed to kill the *Desmodus* that stopped by for its feeding. Ruined a perfectly good rifle, unfortunately." He gestured to his cloak.

"Still, I got a nice cape out of the deal."

"And what does all of this have to do with us," Sam said, speaking up.

Freeborn looked at her. "With you? Nothing." He gestured to Rice and Morgan. "With them? Everything."

"And me?" Orne said.

"Of course darling. You are my help-meet, after all," Freeborn said, stroking the young woman's cheek. "Moreso than some I could name."

Sam made a sound halfway between a laugh and a sigh. "Of course. It's all about your damn research, isn't it?"

"My 'damn research,' as you call it, will revolutionize what we think we know about the history of mankind." Freeborn's face flushed. Jimmy got the feeling that this was an old argument—one that suddenly had a new level of deadliness attached.

"It's all here!" he continued. "Mu! This was an outpost of that long forgotten empire—"

"Oh, twaddle!" Rice said, heaving himself to his feet. "Bunkum! The heat has driven you mad!"

"Mad? Was Armitage mad?" Freeborn said quietly. "Or Peaslee? Or Dyer?"

Rice and Morgan looked at one another. Freeborn smirked. "No. No, I thought not. Can't you see?" He spread his arms. "With your help, we can rewrite the history books!"

"Then why try and kill us?" Jimmy snapped, unable to contain himself. Freeborn looked at him as if only just then remembering that he still existed.

"I thought I explained that. I didn't send them to kill you. I merely asked my men to ensure that no one other than those I had specified came to Ghora. They are an—ah—literal people, I'm afraid."

"Could have fooled me," Jimmy said. "Fine. Now what?"

"Now? Now, you get some rest. We have a busy night ahead of us," Freeborn said, gesturing. Sam and the others, barring Orne, were jerked to their feet by the Ghora. Jimmy started to struggle, but the edge of a sword beneath his Adam's Apple made him freeze.

They were herded into a shack and left there. The door was a curtain of stitched together leather, and two of the masked warriors assumed positions to either side. One by one, Jimmy and the others sat.

"He's madder than a hatter," Rice said slowly.

"No. Just a fool," Morgan said. He leaned back against the wall of the shack. "He can't see anything but his own wants. That's Tyler in a damn nutshell." He looked at Sam. "I'm sorry, Samantha."

"Why? It's hardly your fault," she said. She closed her eyes and stretched out. "I knew what he was when we married. But I loved him. I still love him."

"That why you came?" Jimmy said, staring speculatively at the doorway.

"No. I came to see for myself who he'd choose if he were still alive," she said. "Now I know."

"Bad way to find out," Jimmy said. "Think Orne was in on it?"

"On what? Getting us out here? If she wasn't, then she is now." Morgan folded his arms and closed his eyes. Jimmy snorted and shook his head. She was right, of course. It didn't really matter. Not in the long run. Still, it was a damn shame.

He watched the curtain as the others fell into a fitful sleep. If he could get into the jungle, he was sure he could get back to the plane. But from there, where? The engine was busted and he had zilch so far as weapons. He sighed and closed his eyes.

When he opened them, someone was lighting torches. He awoke the others in turn. "It's night," he said, as Sam looked at him questioningly.

"Indeed it is," Freeborn said, ducking through the curtain and stepping into the shack. "How observant of you, Mr. Dolan. All rested and ready then?"

"Ready for what?" Sam said, getting to her feet.

"For you and Mr. Dolan, I'm afraid it's nothing exciting, my dear," Freeborn said smugly. "You'll be staying here. For a while at least. Professors Rice and Morgan, however...."

Both men stood warily. "What do you want with us, Tyler?" Rice said.

"Easier to show you than to tell you. Come along," Freeborn said, leaving the shack. Jimmy made to follow, but one of the guards shoved him back inside.

"Now what?" Sam said, a few minutes later.

"Why ask me?" Jimmy said.

"I assumed you had a plan."

"Plan?" Jimmy grunted. "We need to get out of here, I know that."

"Brilliant. How?"

"It'll come to me."

They sat in silence for a time. Then Sam said, "Now?"

"Soon," Jimmy said.

"Soon?"

"Sooner if you stop badgering me," Jimmy said, sliding down the wall.

"Well, hurry it up." Sam crouched beside the door, peering out. "They seem agitated."

"Probably worried about those damn bats," Jimmy said. "I know I would be."

"No, it's something else," Sam said, reaching towards the curtain. Hands fastened on her wrist and arm and before she could do more than cry out, she was yanked out of the shack. Jimmy lunged after her, slamming into one of the guards, who drove the flat of his sword into Jimmy's face. Jimmy fell, dazed. Feet cracked against his skull and belly, and he curled up, unable to stand. He heard Samantha cry out as she was dragged away by ululating tribesmen.

Then, suddenly, his attackers were springing away. Something hot and wet washed over Jimmy and he peered up through a swelling eye.

"Khuna?" he said, in shock.

The stocky warrior reached down and jerked Jimmy up. Khuna was covered in welts, bruises, cuts and scrapes, but he was alive, his face split by a tiger's grin. His war-club was coated in blood, and his arm was red to the elbow. Two of Jimmy's attackers were down and dead or dying, their skulls crushed.

"Up, Dolan. There are heads to be cut!"

"I thought you were dead," Jimmy said, stooping to snatch up a fallen club. "When that thing took off...."

"Good ride," Khuna grunted, glaring at the masked warriors approaching them. "I'll tell you about it sometime."

"Over all the drinks I'm gonna buy you," Jimmy said. Then, there was no more time for talking, as a ring of bone and wood closed about them.

Jimmy and Khuna went back-to-back, and Jimmy strained every bit of use out of what limited skills he had with a sword-club. The weapon felt ungodly light in his hand as he slashed out with it, blocking blows and trying to launch some of his own.

Over the heads of his opponents, Jimmy saw Sam being dragged out from under the protective net-canopy and towards a ruined plinth that jutted awkwardly from the slope. Overhead, something shrieked eagerly. "Oh hell," Jimmy said.

Khuna sprang away from him, surprising their opponents by crashing amongst them. "Go, Dolan!"

Jimmy charged forward, bowling his opponents over. Emerging from the tangle of limbs, Jimmy sprinted towards the plinth, swinging his club wildly. The men holding Sam lashed hemp ropes around her, tying her to the stone. Jim hit them as they stepped back, driving the shark-teeth of his weapon into one's back. The man fell with a gurgle, ripping the weapon out of Jimmy's hands.

"Jimmy!" Sam screamed.

Jimmy looked up, and immediately wished he hadn't. The *Gorogoro* dove out of the sky and hit the ground with a thump, its wings folding under it in a way that Jimmy had seen vampire bats do in Central America. It screeched and bounded towards Jimmy, moving in a series of awkward hops. Jimmy threw himself to the ground as the giant bat lunged over him.

He rolled to his feet, trying to spot anything that might serve as a weapon. He heard more telltale thumps behind him, and he spun. More of the great bats galloped towards him, needle fangs flashing.

"Dolan!" Khuna shouted. Jimmy glanced over his shoulder just in time to see the islander tossing him a torch. Jimmy snatched it out of the air and turned back, thrusting the torch forward into the open mouth of one of the bats. It squealed and stumbled, hair crackling. Jimmy moved to Sam's side, swinging the torch to drive back the gathered bats. Khuna moved towards him, carrying two clubs with which he slashed at the beasts.

The islander cut Sam's bonds. "We need to get out of here," he said. She stooped and grabbed a spear, hefting it in two hands.

"Who's arguing?" Jimmy said, hurling the torch at a bat. Several of the beasts bounded past the trio, heading for the altogether easier fare clustered beneath the nets. Men and women screamed as the *Gorogoro* attacked, shrilling hungry cries.

"Up the path!" Jimmy said, shoving Sam along.

"Here," Khuna said, tossing Jimmy a gun belt—*his* gun belt. "Found it while I was sneaking through camp, looking for you."

"Great. Those clubs are all well and good, but I prefer Sam Colt's finest," Jimmy said, checking the clip as they ran. "Any ideas about where we go from here?"

"We find the others," Sam said, pushing past the men. "Tyler took them up into the crater, I'm sure of it!"

"Why in the name of God would he do that?" Jimmy said.

"Who cares? Up is better than down," Khuna said.

"How do you figure?" Jimmy said.

"Bats are all down there."

"Point taken," Jimmy said, looking back.

The village among the ruins was in chaos. The galumphing shapes of the bats moved among the primitive dwellings, attacking anyone they could reach. Someone had knocked over a torch, and flames crawled across several structures, casting an eerie light on the proceedings. Jimmy turned away, feeling sick.

They climbed the path as quickly as they could manage in the dark, pressing themselves tight against the rock face whenever a bat swooped too close. For the most part, the creatures seemed more intrigued by the goings-on below, which was a relief.

They arrived at the lip of the crater sooner than Jimmy figured. He stared at the scene that spread out below him, a low whistle escaping him. "My God."

"This is what he was after," Sam whispered, fingers curling into a fist. She swung her purloined sword up onto her shoulder. "All of this time. It was my money, you know. My money that put him where he needed to be. Paid for his trips. Funded his studies." Her face twisted into a grimace. "And this is what it got us."

Jimmy looked at her, then back at the crater. Carved into the interior walls of the dormant volcano, great square towers rose, like something out of an architect's nightmares. Jimmy blinked, the angles making his eyes water. He'd been to New York a few times and had once gone to the roof of the Waldorf-Anthony Building. It was a similar effect.

"Can't deny it's something," he said after a moment. "Sure looks like a— what'd he call it—outpost of Moo to me."

"Tracks," Khuna said, pointing to the ground.

Jimmy looked up at the sky. There was a slice of orange light on the far horizon. "Sun will be up in an hour or two, and the bats will be coming back. We need to hurry. Come on!"

They set off again, following the path into the Ghoral Crater. The smell of rotten eggs grew, mingling with the ammonia-stink of a bat roost. The path grew narrow and crooked, becoming little more than a downward sloping ledge of crumbling rock.

"Why risk coming here in the dark?" Sam hissed after nearly losing her footing for the third time.

"The bats," Jimmy said. "By the smell, the damn things roost here. He probably wanted to explore without having to worry about disturbing them."

The towers rose around them as they descended. The strange buildings appeared to have been built into the sides of the crater, and there were things that Jimmy thought might have been aqueducts running from building to building.

"What kind of people lived here, I wonder?" Sam said, craning her neck to peer up at the towers. Her voice carried further than seemed possible, startling all three of them.

"My question exactly, dearest Samantha," Freeborn's voice echoed weirdly, bouncing from stone to stone. "You have a depressing habit of turning up at the most inconvenient times, my dear."

The crack of a rifle mingled with his laughter. Jimmy hit Sam at waist-height, bowling her over. Khuna darted in the opposite direction, sword held low.

Another shot split the foul air, kicking up a spray of soil. Jimmy shoved Sam behind a shattered wall and tried to spot the telltale glint of the gun amongst the ridges of the stone beehive that the interior of the crater resembled.

"Sun's coming up, Freeborn," Jimmy shouted. "You know what that means."

"Unfortunately, yes. Luckily, the bats avoid these buildings for the most part, preferring instead to roost in the lava tubes that worm their way through the lower reaches of the crater." His voice seemed to fade and strengthen, as if he were moving. "You are in far more danger than I, out in the open like that."

"Rice? Morgan?" Jimmy called out, ignoring Freeborn's mockery. "Can you hear me?"

No answer.

Sam rose slightly, and Jimmy grabbed at her, trying to pull her back down. Instead, she lunged away from him. Her sword caught the one that had been falling towards his head with a sound like the pealing of a bell. Jimmy twisted in surprise, his Colt thundering.

A wooden mask shattered and the Ghora flipped backwards silently. A second warrior leapt down from the rocks overhead, and Sam stumbled back, nearly tripping over Jimmy. He surged forward, driving his shoulder into the man's chest and driving him back into the rocks. Relentlessly, Jimmy drove his fist into the man's face, cracking the mask, then dislodging it entirely. The native slumped, his face a bloody mess.

"They were waiting for us. He must have had men stationed on the path," Jimmy said, stepping back, his breath coming in harsh pants. He gestured to the path, where it wound down into the crater's depths. "Probably got 'em down there as well. Waiting to pick us off."

"Tyler always made it a point of pride to be two steps ahead," Sam said. "Where's Khuna?"

Jimmy looked around, but there was no sign of the other man. "Damn. He'll be fine." He looked up and saw the sky above the crater turning a light purple. "We need to find a way inside these buildings, and fast."

"Are you serious?"

"Like a heart attack. Unless you prefer the bats?"

Sam frowned and tightened her grip on her sword. Then she brightened. "Those things there. What about them?" She pointed towards the formations Jimmy had taken for aqueducts. They rose away from the ledge and entered the buildings through oddly proportioned culverts. The latter looked just wide enough to accommodate a human body.

Jimmy grinned. "I think I'm falling in love with you."

"You wouldn't be the first." They scrambled towards the closest aqueduct and began to climb. The formations were only wide enough for them to climb one at a time and even then they could only put one foot in front of the other. It took them twenty minutes of muscle-straining exertion to reach the half-way point. Jimmy glanced over the edge and cursed.

Darkness expanded into infinity below them, a vastly wide oblivion that seemed to go on forever. A brief scrap of memory tugged at him, and he remembered his school days, replete with nuns and rulers. He remembered Sister Mary-Louise and her description of what awaited little James Dolan in the afterlife. Hell wasn't bright, she said. It wasn't just fire and fearsome beasties, but a darkness as wide as the world, stretching from pole to pole and reaching down through time itself. Hell was black and empty and right now he thought he might be staring into its open mouth.

"Whatever you do, don't look down," he said.

"What about up?" Sam said, her voice hoarse with fear.

Jimmy looked up. Above them, a swarm of bats circled the mouth of the crater and then flew downwards in a rush as the sun crested the horizon. Their shrieks and howls rebounded from the crater walls like the wails of lost souls, and Jimmy clapped a hand to his ear. "Move! Move!" he shouted.

The great shapes of the bats darted past them, hurtling downwards into the depths of the dormant volcano. Some came so close that the tips of their wings brushed up against Jimmy's shoulders and legs.

One caught Sam on the side of the head, and she slumped sideways, dazed. Jimmy watched in horror as she slipped off of the edge of the aqueduct, and he threw himself forward, his hand shooting out to grab hers. "Hold on!" he shouted, his shoulder muscles screaming as he flattened himself on the stone. Despite his body's protests, he hauled the woman up to safety.

"Go!" he snapped, then turned, extending his pistol.

"But—"

"Go, damn it, *go!*"

The giant bat skittered towards him, jaws agape, eyes gleaming hungrily. Jimmy fell onto his back and clutched his pistol in both hands, firing as the bat launched itself at him. Its weight caused the aqueduct to wobble, and Jimmy scooted backwards, firing again. The bat gave a scream and flopped off, tumbling into the abyss, but too late.

Stone cracked and shifted. Jimmy turned and clawed for safety as the aqueduct began to give way. Sam's hand found his just as the aqueduct collapsed from beneath him, and he clambered into the culvert, his heels sliding on the polished stone.

They crouched there for a moment, listening to the sounds of falling stone and shrieking bats. Jimmy looked at Sam, who smiled. "One good turn deserves another, right?" she said.

"Who's keeping count?" Jimmy said. "How far does this thing go?"

"Only one way to find out, I suppose," she said, turning and squirming up into the sluice. It was a precarious climb. The stone had been polished smooth by whatever liquid had once run through it, and there were precious few places to grip with either fingers or toes.

They climbed for what seemed like hours, until Sam stopped at a narrow bend. "Give me a boost," she said, craning her neck to peer at Jimmy through her spread limbs. "I think I spotted a way out."

"You sure?"

"Sure, I'm sure. It looks like a sluice-gate."

"You better be right about this. I'm a small guy, but this is getting ridiculous," Jimmy said, and he braced himself as well as he was able. "I'm getting cramps in my cramps." With a grunt, he placed his palms beneath her feet and shoved her upwards. She disappeared with a yelp. Jimmy stretched, reaching up a hand. "Once you get situated, give me a hand would ya?"

Sam grabbed his wrist and pulled, and Jimmy squeezed his bulk up through the sluice-gate. "Ease up on the grip, lady. I ain't made out of steel," he groused, as her grip tightened like a vise. However, as he worked himself free of the tiny opening, he suddenly realized that it wasn't Sam who had a grip on his arm after all.

Wooden bat-masks glared down at him, and a rifle jabbed him in the ribs. Jimmy sighed in disgust and raised his hands.

"Crap."

"He threw himself forward…"

"Not at all. Quite impressive really," Freeborn said, standing across the room, his arms wrapped around Sam, holding her immobile. Rice and Morgan both stood nearby, ringed about by masked warriors. Orne stood a little way from them, holding her rifle loosely. "I fully expected you to die, not find your way here, to the very heart of the matter."

"We don't always get what we want, I guess," Jimmy said, as one of his captors took his pistol and tossed it back down through the hole he'd just exited.

"No. We don't." Freeborn shoved Sam forward, into Jimmy's arms. "You can have her, though. If you'd like."

"Tyler, you sonnuva—" Sam began, as Jimmy grabbed her before she could lunge back at her husband.

Freeborn chuckled and spread his hands. "Tut-tut. No sense ruining this moment with nastiness, now is there?"

"What are you talking about?" Jimmy said, quietly gauging how close he could get to Freeborn before the Ghora stopped him. However far it was, it probably wasn't going to be close enough. He needed to keep the man talking.

"I'm talking about this feat of ancient architectural skill you find yourself standing in, Mr. Dolan. Doesn't it just take your breath away?" Freeborn turned in a slow circle, gesturing to the walls and the floor. There was a strange mosaic covering a section of the latter, filthy but still visible. The walls were covered in black mold and strange shapes that hurt Jimmy's eyes.

"No. But the volcanic gas and the bat-reek sure as heck does," Jimmy said. "Smells like a dead horse in here."

"Yes. Well, small minds make for small senses, as they say," Freeborn said. "You might be interested to know the purpose of those flues you crawled up, eh?"

"Not really," Jimmy said.

"Troughs, Mr. Dolan. Feeding troughs, for the bats. I believe the long-gone inhabitants of this city fed them. For what purpose, I cannot say. Perhaps the beasts come by their love of human meat honestly."

"Wonderful." Jimmy looked around. "Find of the damn century."

"Warren, be a pal and tell them what you found," Freeborn said, still playing the diligent professor.

"Tyler, please," Rice said. "Let's just get out of here."

"No!" Freeborn whipped around, the edge of his cloak flaring as he jabbed a finger at his former colleagues. "I'm not leaving here until I have what I want!"

"And what the hell is that? You've got the damn city, isn't that enough?" Jimmy snarled.

"Not by a long shot," Orne said, speaking up. She stepped forward, smiling crookedly. "You don't get it, do you, you dumb brute?"

"Maybe if you use fewer syllables," Jimmy said, grinning at her. "Babe."

Orne growled and raised her rifle, as if to crack the butt into Jimmy's face. He tensed, but Freeborn raised a hand.

"The city was easy enough to find, Mr. Dolan. Anyone could have done that, if they'd bothered to look closely. No, it's what the city represents...." Freeborn took off his mask and smiled. "Do you think this is the first time I've been here? I've come here every night for a year, studying the runes, sigils and bas-reliefs decorating every inch of this place." He gestured, indicating the strange shapes that decorated the dark walls. Jimmy squinted, trying to discern what they were, but gave up after a moment. If it wasn't route charts or dirty magazines, it wasn't worth trying to read, in his book.

"So, what, you got eyestrain?" he said.

Freeborn snapped his fingers and a club caught Jimmy in the side, driving him to his knees. Gagging, Jimmy glared at the other man.

"In a way. There are limits to my knowledge, even with what gleanings I gathered from the Ponape Scriptures," Freeborn said, and Rice made a sound that might have been a moan. "But with my good friends, Warren and Francis here...."

"This is madness!" Morgan exploded. He jerked forward, and two of the Ghora grabbed his arms before he could make a move. "Madness!"

"Only if I fail." He raised his arms and smiled widely. "You see, thanks to my former colleagues, I have discovered that this city, Mr. Dolan, is but the merest fragment of something greater! The merest fingertip of a titan hand! The city was not built on the island, the *island grew around the city!*" He laughed wildly. "I suspected before, but now I have confirmation!"

Jimmy got to his feet. "That supposed to impress me?"

"Of course not." Freeborn calmed himself abruptly. "Now this—*this* is supposed to impress you: I'm going to sink the island."

Jimmy blinked. "What?"

"Further down," Rice said, haltingly. "Massive engines. Gears and cogs and...things." He closed his eyes and slumped, held up by one of the Ghora.

Freeborn wiggled his fingers and smiled. "Like a drawbridge going up and down. Stimulate the system, and down we go, back into—"

"The heart of the volcano!" Jimmy said. "They were right, Freeborn. You're nuttier than fruitcake at Christmas! Even if you were right, the odds of getting something like that to work now...."

"Just imagine it!" Orne said, eyes blazing with the fervor of the converted. "A whole city...perhaps lost Mu itself!"

"Imagine what secrets it holds," Freeborn said softly. "What powers...it's the floor. The mosaic. Press the tiles in the right pattern and these towers should descend." He smiled at Rice. "That's what Warren says, at any rate. Hopefully, his command of the primitive Naacal tongue is still up to snuff, eh Mr. Dolan?"

"Nuts to you!" Jimmy said. "What about those people out there? What happens to them when you do this?"

"Savages." Freeborn made a dismissive gesture. "Pathetic, degraded cannibals." He gestured and one of his men grabbed Morgan and shoved him forward. "This room is the control center, isn't it Francis? Just as Warren said. And you can see how to make it work."

Morgan glared at him silently. Jimmy tensed. Whatever was coming wasn't going to be good. Freeborn pulled a stone dagger from his belt and pressed it to Morgan's throat. "You can read the signs there, on the floor. Make it work, Francis, and you can share the glory. You and Warren. Refuse, and I'll feed you both to the bats, piece by quivering piece."

"Go to hell," Morgan said.

Freeborn closed his eyes. Then he opened them and sighed. "You first."

The report of a pistol echoed loudly in the chamber. Freeborn yelped as the knife flew from his hand, along with one of his fingers.

Khuna, crouched in one of the high, featureless windows, looked at Jimmy. "Two you owe me, Dolan," he said, waving his Webley.

"Add it to the tab!" Jimmy said, swinging his arms out into the bellies of the two warriors standing to either side of him. They doubled over with twin gasps of pain. Jimmy twisted, grabbing one around the neck, and spun, shoving the dazed warrior headfirst into the sluice-gate!

As he disappeared from sight with only a despairing shriek to mark his passage, his companion swung his tooth-studded club at Jimmy.

Sam caught the Ghora in the side with her shoulder, knocking him off balance. Jimmy caught the club on his forearm, grunting as the limb went numb from the force of the blow, and drove his fist into the man's throat. The Ghora staggered, choking. Jimmy locked his fists and brought them both down on the back of the man's neck.

As his opponent fell, Jimmy saw that the other guards were busy with

Rice and Morgan, who had taken the opportunity to hurl themselves at the Ghora. Orne was backing away from the ruckus, raising her rifle.

"Stay back! Stay back!" she shouted. Khuna paced towards her, grinning with feral intensity.

Jimmy bounded towards Freeborn, who was already staggering away, clutching his wounded hand. "Leaving so soon?" he said, grabbing onto the back of the man's cloak. He jerked at it, and Freeborn stumbled backwards. A flailing hand caught Jimmy on the side of the head. Freeborn twisted like a snake, kicking Jimmy's knee and knocking him off of his feet.

Then Freeborn was moving again, running out of the room and into the maze of corridors beyond. Jimmy snarled and loped after him.

"Get back here, Freeborn!"

He pursued the other man through the halls and up a flight of curving stairs that at last opened out onto a rooftop plaza. Broken columns and empty plinths littered the space. Freeborn backed away, face twisted into a rictus of hatred.

"Idiot. Idiot! You're ruining everything!"

"Bet you wish your boys had got me in Motugra now, huh?" Jimmy said, pounding his fist into his palm. "I don't get it…all of this, and for what? Some old ruins? Hell, I'd have tried exporting the guano, at least!"

"Money? You think this was about money?" Freeborn said. "This was about leaving a trail of fire across the history of the world!" He pointed his bloody hand at Jimmy. "This was about cracking open the Earth itself and reading its entrails!"

"Sounds great. This here, though?" Jimmy said pointing to a spot between them. "This is about beating the crap out of you before I drag you back to the plane."

"No," Freeborn said, turning and sprinting for the edge of the roof. Jimmy blinked in surprise, then followed him. He tackled Freeborn and they rolled across the roof, coming dangerously close to the edge.

An elbow caught Jimmy in the chest and he rolled away, coughing. Freeborn rose into a crouch and sprang, jamming his bloody fingers into Jimmy's face, blinding him.

"I will find what lies beneath!" Freeborn howled, grabbing Jimmy's throat and squeezing with frenzied strength. Jimmy clawed at his wrists, trying to break their hold, but Freeborn only redoubled his efforts. "The secrets of Mu will be mine! *Mine!*"

"You—ack—can have 'em!" Jimmy said, punching Freeborn in the kidney and belly, trying to dislodge him. Freeborn let go and staggered upright, wheezing.

"Mine—" he said.

The bat hit him like a cannonball. Jimmy could only lie there and watch as Tyler Freeborn was carried off the roof and out over the abyss by the *Gorogoro*. The creature swooped downwards with a single whip-crack of its wings, descending into the darkness below, carrying Freeborn with it.

Jimmy climbed slowly to his feet, feeling the aches and pains of his recent exertions come crashing onto him all at once. He looked up at the circle of sunlight far above, then staggered towards the stairs as quickly as possible.

"Jimmy!" Sam said, meeting him at the bottom of the stairs. "What happened? Where's Tyler?"

"Gone," Jimmy said as she caught him before he could fall. "I would like to be paid now, please."

The bats had retreated to the depths with the coming of the morning, and the slopes were clear of human-sized trouble. Arm around Sam's shoulders, Jimmy looked at the wrecked village and shook his head.

"Think they're all dead?"

"No." Morgan said, holding Orne's rifle in the crook of his arms. "But they'll be avoiding the crater for a while, I'll bet."

"Which is a good thing, right?" Jimmy said.

"Best thing for everyone concerned," Rice said. "I, personally, am all for forgetting this place even exists."

"You can't hide this," Orne said sullenly. "Not forever."

Jimmy glanced at her. "Lady, I could care less whether you forget about it or open a damn theme park. All I want now is to go home, have a hot bath and cold drink, possibly not in that order."

"Amen," Rice said, slapping Jimmy on the shoulder. Jimmy winced. "Amen to that."

It took them a day to get back to the beach, and they were a sorry bunch on arrival. A brightly painted rumrunner sat in the lagoon, engine idling, and a man sat on the back, fishing.

"That you, Dolan?" he shouted, upon sighting them with his one good eye. The other was hidden behind an eye patch, which went well with the navy captain's hat perched on his head.

"Depends. That you, Fortune?" Jimmy shouted back.

"You're late. I've been waiting here for ages," Nick Fortune said. "Tow cable is all hooked up and ready to go."

"You'll live." Jimmy looked up at the sky, which was growing dark.

"Provided that we get out of here as soon as possible."

As Fortune's boat chugged out of the lagoon, Jimmy looked back at the crater where it thrust upward out of the jungle. As he watched, winged shapes exploded out into the darkening sky and swirled upwards in a typhoon of leather and teeth.

"They're almost pretty, from a distance," Sam murmured, leaning against him.

"I don't know, I think I see something a whole lot better a whole lot closer to hand," Jimmy said, looking down at her. Sam looked up at him, and Jimmy leaned down, eyes closed.

"Really? Honestly?"

Jimmy's eyes popped open. Sam grinned. "My husband *just* died, Mr. Dolan."

"Jeeez, Jimmy," Fortune said from somewhere below. "Talk about premature."

Khuna said something in his own language, which made Fortune howl with laughter. Soon, the others had joined in.

"Ah shut up, the whole lot of ya," Jimmy growled, dropping his chin into his hands. Somewhere, a bat shrieked.

Jimmy thought he knew just how it felt.

The End

WHY'D IT HAVE TO BE BATS, YOU ASK?

Why not?

There are stories about giant bats in every part of the world that has bats, which is, in effect, every part of the world. There are bats in the jungles, the mountains, the snowy peaks and the humid valleys. They roost in volcanoes, sea-caves, urban wastelands and rural idylls. Everywhere we are, they are. Ubiquitous and unseen.

Scientists figure that in a few thousand years, they'll be among the top-five competing species, alongside rats and cockroaches. Archaeologists and biologists have found evidence that some species of bat were as big as dogs and possibly treated as gods or demons. There's a reason that bat-gods are prevalent in certain cultures and that bats frighten us even now.

Truth be told, this story wasn't very hard to write.

Five minutes on Google, and I had the bare bones of the thing well and truly uncovered. A day or four after that, and it was written. I'm almost ashamed to say it, but I spent roughly eight hours, all told, on this one, start to finish. I don't know whether that's good or bad, but I'll leave it up to you to judge. I wrote it to order, imagining what would make a good illustration or cover image for one of those old yellowed men's adventure magazines in the truest tradition of the pulps, and I hope you enjoy it.

JOSHUA M. REYNOLDS is a freelance writer of moderate skill and exceptional confidence. He has written a bit, and some of it was even published. For money. By real people. His work has appeared in anthologies such as *Cthulhu Unbound 2*, and in periodicals such as *Innsmouth Free Press*.

Feel free to stop by his blog, [http://joshuamreynolds.blogspot.com/] and cast aspersions on his character.

THE EYE OF KA
By Bill Craig

On an island somewhere in the South Sea...
The sun was blazing hot overhead in a nearly cloudless blue sky. The waters surrounding the island were a deep cerulean blue. Every leaf in the jungle seemed to stand out in stark relief against the foliage behind it. A dragonfly buzzed past the leaves that were stirring in the breeze.

Suddenly shouts shattered the easy silence, with the sound of something or someone crashing through the underbrush. A man charged into view, wearing a battered leather jacket and a faded brown fedora. A green canvas bag hung from his right shoulder to his left hip. Three spears flashed past him and he spun, drawing and firing a revolver back in the directions from which the spears came. There were more shouts and a cry of pain, but the man paid it no heed, spinning and heading for an opening in the trees.

He could see a dock stretching out into the blue water and at the end of the dock a boat that was just getting ready to pull away from the dock. The man ran faster, charging out of the jungle and onto the dock with spears stabbing into the wooden boards behind him. The guy on the boat had untied the last line and was almost back to the pilothouse as the man in the jacket and hat leaped off the dock and landed on the deck with a thud that rocked the boat.

The captain spun to see what had happened; he saw the man and then looked at the dock that was rapidly filling with angry islanders. He hit the throttle and smoke belched from the smoke stack as the engine roared and the boat sped away from shore.

"Permission to come aboard?" the stranger asked. The boat captain looked him up and down.

"Isn't it a little late to ask?" the captain pulled off his cap and ran his fingers through his thick brown hair. The captain was nearly six feet tall with a longshoreman's build. His hands were calloused and his knuckles bore the scars of numerous fights. His skin was sun-bronzed and his single eye glinted like a bright blue marble in the sun. A black patch covered the other one.

"I was in a bit of a hurry. It didn't seem like a good idea to hang around. Name's Burke. I'm an archeologist," the man introduced himself.

"Nick Fortune, owner and Captain of Fortune's Folly," the captain introduced himself.

"Where are you headed, Nick?"

"Motugra, to collect for the supplies that I dropped off for the trading post back there. I guess it may be a while before I'm hired to make another run there," Nick shook his head.

"Sorry about that. Guy that dropped me off wasn't going to be back for a week. You don't know how much I appreciate you getting me outta there. Those fellas wanted to kill me," Burke sighed heavily.

"And just why is that?" Fortune turned his head to look at him.

"I guess they don't like people going inside their old temples," Burke shrugged.

"Let me guess, they didn't know you were on the island until they caught you in the temple or coming out of it?" Nick asked.

"Something like that," Burke sat down on the deck and leaned back on the gunwale, sweat dripping down his face. Pretty soon his head was nodding and the man fell asleep. Nick shook his head, knowing that there was a lot more to the story than what Burke was telling him. He made a mental note to talk to Jimmy Dolan if he was on Motugra, figuring it was likely Dolan who had dropped Burke off on the island.

Of course, if Dolan was on the island, he was probably in the Hanging Monkey. At the very least, Nick knew he would leave a message with Corky O'Brian for Jimmy to find him. Burke would bear watching. There was something about the guy that Nick just didn't like. Burke was snoring loud enough that Nick could hear him over the engine. He looked at his watch. It would take a couple of hours to reach Motugra. Nick dug a wrinkled pack of Lucky Strikes out of his shirt pocket and shook one out. He pulled out a beat-up Zippo lighter and fired up his smoke. It was a beautiful day to be on the ocean. *Kinda like old times, before prohibition. God what a mess that had been. Joanie.* Nick blinked back tears, forcing the memory away. It was still too much: the memories. *No,* he shook his head, pushing them away as he watched dolphins jumping and playing to port, chaperoning him back to Motugra.

※ ※ ※

Grace Thomas was sitting in the Hanging Monkey sipping at a cup of coffee and reading an Australian newspaper left behind by a passing sailor. Grace had platinum blonde hair drawn back in a ponytail, with a few pin curls around her face. She had on a pillbox cap and a smartly tailored jacket and skirt over a white blouse and heels. Her shapely legs were covered in silk with a seam that ran up the back.

She looked up as Corky O'Brian entered the main room from his office in the back. Grace waved him over. "So where is Nick Fortune hiding these days, Corky?"

"Nick is his own man, Grace. I don't keep track of him. Why do you ask?" the Irishman looked at her. He had long wondered what her interest in the Italian American sailor was.

"But aren't you his best friend?" Grace smiled, and Corky felt his indifference wavering.

"That I am, but Nick is a man who likes his privacy, and I am not one to tell tales out of school," Corky smiled at her, his teeth white and even in his freckled face. His curly red hair was an unruly mess on his head.

"Has Jimmy been in? I heard he had an interesting charter the other day," Grace looked at him batting her lashes. Corky smiled despite himself. He liked this girl's spirit; however, he knew that she meant something to Nick Fortune despite Nick's protest to the contrary.

Jimmy Dolan was also a friend of Nick's as well as a friendly competitor. Jimmy was a pilot and transported both people and supplies, just as Nick did on his boat. However, if either was in trouble, the other would quickly come running.

"Jimmy blows in like the wind, much the same as Nick, Grace. You be knowing that. To hear you tell it, you barely know the habits of either and you got here not long after them. Don't try to kid a kidder, Grace. Just be honest with your questions," Corky winked at her.

"You take good care of them both, don't you, Corky?" Grace smiled at him.

"Someone has to, lassie," Corky grinned. "Else they might fall captive to your considerable charms."

"Why Corky, I do believe that's the nicest thing you've ever said to me," Grace batted her eyelashes at him and smiled, and once more Corky felt himself wavering. Then there was a commotion at the door and an angry patron stomped in.

"That damned beast stole the very hat off ma head and then put it on and hung there in the branches laughing at me," Poke Doohan roared as he stomped his way to the bar.

"An' what beastie was that?" Corky raised an eyebrow.

"That damned Monkey that always hangs about outside watching the place," Doohan groaned.

"And what would he be wanting with that rag you call a hat? I'd be thinking even a jungle beast would have better taste than that," Corky roared with laughter. The hat in question was a beat up bowler that the Scottish Banker had worn far past its prime. Personally, Corky felt as if the Monkey had done the whole island a service by stealing it.

"Miko, set Doohan up a round and we'll put it on the Monkey's tab. After all, the primate has done us all a service in that we will never have to see that damned hat again," Corky yelled to the Chinese bartender.

"O'Brian, that beast is a menace, I tell you," Doohan started.

"Then tell Colonel Smythe about it on his next pass through," Corky scoffed, referring to the British colonel who provided policing for the islands in the Motugra chain.

"Perhaps I can get the bloody Brit to shoot the bloody beast," Doohan replied.

"Hey, Doohan," A voice called from the doorway. The mayor of the small city stood there holding the battered bowler.

"How did you get me bloody hat back from yon wee beastie?" Doohan asked, shocked that the mayor had it.

"He gave it to me to give back to you," Mayor Roger Cadderly replied with quiet dignity. Doohan lumbered over and snatched it from the mayor's hand and plopped it down on his head. Suddenly Doohan made a face.

"What the hell?" Doohan roared, tearing the hat off his head and looking down into it. His hair was covered by a liquidy brown substance. "The damn beastie crapped in my hat!" The bar exploded in laughter. Doohan stomped out in a snit.

"There is a story for ye, lass," Corky chuckled.

"Local Banker terrorized by wild monkey. Yes, that would certainly be a headline to raise the eyebrows back in America," Grace Thomas laughed, the sound almost musical. "Except exactly how would I say what the monkey had done?" Grace looked at him.

"I'm sure ye kin find the proper words, Lass," Corky grinned again.

"Perhaps, though it isn't exactly the type of story I'm looking for," Grace smiled almost seductively.

"And what kind would that be, Gracie?" Corky looked at her intently.

"A story with mystery and intrigue, perhaps even one with murder,"

Grace smiled back, her eyes sparkling.

"Good luck with that, Gracie," Corky smiled and then turned and walked back to his office.

Grace Thomas watched him go. There was more there than met the eye so far as that crazy Irishman was concerned. She could tell that. In his own way he was as much a mystery as Nick Fortune and Jimmy Dolan. They were three very different men, but in many ways, they were all very much alike. They all covered for one another in many ways. They were in effect an Old Boys Club to which she could never gain membership.

Nick Fortune liked her. It was evident in the looks he gave her, despite the natural wariness that crept into his eyes whenever they talked. Nick was a man with secrets. Secrets that he had buried deep, so deep he would never want to see them come to light. But they were secrets that she wanted to know.

She found the man enticing and exciting all at once. There was an aura of mystery about him, mixed with an aura of danger. Yes, Nick Fortune was a man that she definitely wanted to know far better than she already did....

Nick Fortune spotted the channel markers that would guide him into Motugra Bay. It was one of the few deep water ports in the island chain and as such made it a shipping port for cargo coming in and going out of the islands. It had seemed a good place to get away from it all when he had left New York. There had been too many memories there—too much that he had wanted nothing more than to walk away from, to forget. The journey hadn't been an easy one, and not without costs. He touched the eye patch. Sometimes he still felt pains in the empty socket.

Nick spun the wheel, turning the old rum runner into the channel to head for the docks. Memories flooded his mind. A fog-shrouded night on the Hudson River; boats flying around, gunfire tearing the night apart;. Joanie on the bridge, ducking beneath the hail of gunfire, sweeping her blonde hair from her face as the salt spray wetted it down.

Nick had been on the front of the boat, firing guns at the boats that were attacking them. Some claimed to be federal authorities, but Nick doubted it, believing them to be nothing more than bootleggers after the whiskey that he was transporting in to his uncle, John Fortunelli.

A bullet had found Joanie, and she had fallen to the deck, her crimson blood spreading over her blouse and the deck. Fortune had dropped to his knees beside her, tears flowing from his eyes. Joanie had grasped his hand as life had expired from her body. Fortune had rolled her over the side of the boat into the surf. At that moment he had decided to leave....

Nick blinked back the tears that had come unbidden to his eye. He had left New York to try to forget that awful night, to leave it as far behind as he had the rest of his past. But that night, he could not get out of his head. He pulled out his crumpled pack of cigarettes and shook out a Lucky Strike. He lit it and exhaled smoke, letting the breeze carry it away. What a morning it had been. He shook his head.

Jimmy Dolan had climbed high as he had approached the island of Motugra. These days there were too many enemies crawling about, what with the Japanese and the Germans moving into the islands. Not to mention the usual sky pirates who would just as soon shoot a man down as look at him if they got a chance at the cargo he was carrying. No, better to come down out of the sun where no one would see him 'til it was too late. It was a trick he had learned with the Flying Tigers over China.

Jimmy chewed an unlit cigar stub as the plane dropped quickly out of the sky to glide smoothly to a landing on the calm waters of Motugra Bay. The Goose cut across the smooth calm water like a knife, heading straight for the docks. He had spotted Fortune's Folly just entering the Bay and wanted to be waiting inside the Hanging Monkey when his friend got there.

Even Jimmy had to admit that Nick Fortune was something of a man of mystery. Nick rarely talked about his past and then only when they were alone. He knew that Nick was an Italian American originally from New York but very little beyond that except that he was a hard working man who feared nothing. Nick never even talked about how he lost his eye. Nick made decent money hauling cargo between the islands and sometimes they competed for it, but their friendship remained strong despite the competition.

Occasionally Jimmy took the odd government job, checking out locations where the Germans and Japanese had started building a presence. The British and American governments both paid well for such information and Jimmy felt obliged to provide his services, but he never turned down the paycheck. Nick said Jimmy had a mercenary soul, but was still a patriot. Jimmy agreed with him.

Jimmy had seen something coming in over one of the lesser islands that he wanted to get together with Nick and check out. He still had a day before he was supposed to meet back up with the guy he had dropped off over on Papogo Island. He shook his head. Burke had been a real piece of work.

The man claimed to be an archeologist, but Dolan had the feeling that he was nothing but a tomb raider and that the cannibals on Papogo would make short work of him. However, the man paid in cash and cash was king. His mechanic, Jake Sloan, was on the dock to greet him and quickly got the amphibious plane tied up to the dock.

Dolan was out of the hatch as soon as the props stopped turning, more than willing to turn his baby over to the mechanic that kept her going. "Hey, Boss," Jake called, waving.

"Hey, Jake," Dolan called as his feet hit the dock.

"How was your trip?" Jake asked.

"The usual," Jimmy waved him off as he walked away.

Nick Fortune watched as Jimmy Dolan's plane sliced across the bay heading for the docks. Dolan would be gone before he got tied up, but Nick knew he could find the pilot later at the Hanging Monkey. He had some questions for him about his passenger and what the man was doing on Papogo Island in the first place. Fortune knew he could search the man and find out, but he wasn't ready to make waves yet just on suspicion.

Things were happening in the outside world and, if the rumors were true, the world was headed back to war again. It saddened Nick because he had come to the South Seas to forget about the outside world. However, it seemed as though the outside world didn't want to let him forget. Nick shot a glance over his shoulder at his passenger. The so-called archeologist was still sawing logs.

Nick lit another Lucky as he guided the boat across the bay towards the docks. He had a bad feeling about Burke. The man was an ill omen of some sort, and evil seemed to hang over him like a cloud. Nick exhaled a cloud of smoke and dismissed the thought. It wouldn't do to think too strongly on it. Sailors are a superstitious lot, and Nick was no different. Thinking about evil could draw it to you and he had no desire for that. He had traveled too far to avoid it to invite more evil into his life!

Jimmy Dolan swaggered into the Hanging Monkey as if he owned the place. He was feeling good and it felt good to be back on the island he called home. The bar was doing a booming business, full of sailors and merchant seamen as well as a few military people. Corky O'Brian nodded as he saw Dolan enter and the ace pilot made his way across the crowded floor.

"Corky, lad, set me up will ye?" Dolan called as he approached the bar. Two men at a nearby table eyed him closely. Dolan paid them no mind for he was used to such looks and they bothered him not at all.

"Jimmy, lad, how have you been?" Corky asked, sending the two men a hard look that let them know that Dolan was not without friends in the Hanging Monkey.

"Has Nick been in yet? I need to talk to him about something."

Dolan grabbed a mug and sipped at the brew within it. He smacked his lips afterwards, signaling his approval.

"Not yet, but he should be coming soon," O'Brian replied.

"Glad to hear it! This is a fair day, my friend," Dolan grinned as he swilled his beer.

"That it is, lad. The monkey stole Doohan's hat and took a crap in it. You should have seen the look on the banker's face when he put it on his head. The Mayor himself handed the hat to Doohan and I can't but wonder if Cadderly hadn't paid the damn chimp to do it," Corky confided.

"I can't say it would surprise me a bit. There's no love lost between the two of them," Jimmy Dolan threw back his head and roared with laughter. He grabbed his mug and took a deep drink, smacking his lips loudly afterwards. The two men that had been watching him from the other table stood and walked towards them.

Both of them were fairly stout fellows with thick necks and bulging biceps. Both of them had low foreheads and thick brows with slightly crooked noses. Their scarred knuckles were testament to the brawls they had been in. Their red and white striped shirts were stretched taut across muscular chests. That they were looking for trouble was a given. They just didn't know how much they had found!

"You are too loud!" one of the men said in a thickly accented voice.

"Mate, head back to your seat, now!" Corky O'Brian ordered, his tone steel-coated.

"No," the other man grinned evilly, revealing uneven teeth.

"Is that right?" Corky asked, smiling. The bar owner stood up. His fist closed over the long neck of the beer bottle on the table. Jimmy was on his feet as well.

One of the men drew back his fist and Corky shattered the bottle across his nose, drawing a scream of pain. While the second man was distracted, Jimmy smashed the heavy glass mug of beer into his face. The mug exploded into shards of glass and foam, burning the man's eyes. Dolan kicked him in the groin hard enough to lift him off his feet and the man fell to the floor in a fetal position, his hands between his legs, making pitiful mewling sounds.

The man Corky had hit launched a roundhouse kick that caught the ex-pat Irishman in the gut and sent him stumbling backwards. Corky roared in anger and threw himself at the man. A hard knuckled fist lashed out and caught the man in both gut and on the point of his chin, dropping him to the floor. Two other men thought to get in on the action, and, when they caught the gaze of the Irishman and the American, thought better of it. They sat back down as a large native islander walked over and took the unconscious sailors by the collar and dragged them out of the bar. Dolan looked at the Irishman.

"Damn if that didn't make me thirsty," Dolan announced.

"Breathing makes you thirsty, Jimmy," Corky laughed.

"That it does, old friend, that it does," Dolan roared his laughter.

Burke opened his eyes, having felt the boat slow. He knew they were pulling into port. The Captain made him nervous. He seemed like the curious type, and it wouldn't do for him to get too curious about what Burke had removed from the island. Burke thought about his gun, but then decided it would not be a good idea. Based on the shouts he was hearing, the Captain was well known in this port and, if something happened, there would be folks looking into it. That was never good.

Burke made a production out of yawning and stretching, loud enough that Fortune heard him. He saw the man glance over his shoulder. For the moment, Fortune and Jimmy Dolan were both loose ends. He would have to do something about both before he left Motugra. Given the treasure he had recovered, he could afford to leave no living witnesses!

Grace Thomas sat in front of the mirror, brushing her hair. Corky could be infuriating when she asked about Nick. There was something tragic about Nick Fortune and it hung over him like a cloud, drawing her to him like a moth to a flame. Normally he was not her type, but the air of tragedy that hovered around him suggested that Nick Fortune had a story to tell, and she wanted to be the first to hear it and then to tell it.

Grace smiled at her reflection. She had cabled New York asking for background on the cargo captain but still had not as yet gotten a response. She wondered how long it would take, given the isolation of the small South Sea Island chain.

Nick Fortune was heading up the dock towards the small cabana he rented from Corky O'Brian when Mortimer Collins waved him over. Collins ran the cable office that handled the outside communication between the island and the rest of the world, at least other than when mail came in by boat from Australia or New Zealand.

"Hey, Mort," Nick spoke around the cigarette dangling from the corner of his mouth.

"Nick, you might have some trouble coming," Mort Collins ran a trembling hand through his thinning blond hair. Mort was a small-built man who looked perpetually frail. His clothing always seemed too big and he seemed uncomfortable around other people. He had few friends, but Nick Fortune was definitely one of them.

"Why is that, Mort?" Nick's face never changed expression and there was no outward sign he was even concerned.

"That reporter woman sent a cable to New York City asking about you. She got a couple of replies back, and I don't like the sound of them," Mort shook his head.

"You let her know you got replies back?" Nick took another puff on his Lucky Strike.

"Not yet. I wanted to talk to you and let you see 'em first," Mort shook his head.

"Thank you, my friend. Let's head over to your office and see what they say," Nick put his arm around Mort's shoulders and they headed for the cable office. Mort unlocked the door and ushered Nick inside. Nick closed the door behind them as Mort dialed the combination on the safe and removed the cables. He handed them to Nick. Fortune read the first one.

```
YOUR NICK FORTUNE MAYBE RELATED TO MOBSTER
STOP BE EXTREMELY CAREFUL STOP WANTED FOR
QUESTIONING IN THE DEATH OF JOAN MULGREW AND
DANE CARTER STOP
```

"...you might have trouble coming."

Nick sighed heavily and put his smoke out in the nearly overflowing ashtray. He looked at Mort. His friend was looking off into a corner. Nick looked at the second cable.

```
DESCRIPTION FITS NICHOLAS FORTUNELLI STOP
WANTED FOR QUESTIONING IN AN OPEN MURDER
CASE STOP FBI SENDING SOMEONE TO VERIFY ID
STOP GOOD JOB STOP
```

"Go ahead and deliver them, Mort. It was gonna catch up to me sooner or later," Nick sighed.

"Did you really kill them folks, Nick?" Mort asked softly.

"I did Dane Carter after finding out he was the one that opened fire on my boat and killed Joanie. He had it coming," Nick replied.

"I reckon he did. If I get any word of this G-man, I'll let you know," Mort smiled.

"Thanks, my friend," Nick Fortune headed for his cabana.

Grace Thomas had just finished dressing for the evening when there was a knock at her door. She picked up the snub-nosed .38 revolver and carried it with her as she went to answer the door. Motugra was not the safest place in the world and it didn't pay for a girl to take unnecessary chances. She stood a little to the side of the door and called out. "Who is it?"

"Mortimer Collins, Miss Thomas. I got replies for you from the cables you sent out," came the reply.

"Thank you," Grace replied. She opened the door and the skinny little radioman stood there holding two envelopes. He handed them to her. Grace gave him a five dollar bill. Collins thanked her and disappeared down the walkway that surrounded the residential hotel. She closed and locked the door and carried the two yellow envelopes back to her bed.

Both held replies to the cables she had sent out. The question was: did she really want to know the answers? She was torn. She wanted to know all there was about Nick Fortune, but at the same time, since she had arrived on Motugra, she had developed feelings for him. She wasn't sure if she would call it love; not yet. But she had come to care deeply for the sad-eyed boat captain. Grace took a deep breath and tore open the first envelope.

Burke had gotten himself cleaned up and was headed for the main drinking establishment on Motugra, a bar and restaurant known to one and all as the Hanging Monkey. From what he had learned from listening and asking around the small town both Jimmy Dolan and Nick Fortune frequented the tavern. It would giv,e him the opportunity to deal with the loose ends. He didn't want anyone to know he had the jewel from the idol. The Eye of Ka, it was called.

The jewel was rumored to possess supernatural powers. The Germans had offered him a great deal of money to find it. Their agent was supposed to meet him at the Hanging Monkey. Burke looked forward to collecting. It had been several months since he had drawn a regular salary from the University. Not since that Jones fellow had exposed his artifacts as brilliant fakes. One of these days he would catch up to Jones as well, and when he did…he let the thought go unfinished.

Corky O'Brian drained his shot of whiskey. What a day it had been! The brawl earlier with Dolan had been invigorating, to say the least! He always enjoyed it when Dolan flew in. Nick was fun but lacked the exuberance of the Scottish-American Pilot.

"The men are back," Khuna said.

"Throw them out," Corky replied.

"Yes Boss," the native islander replied.

Cor,ky smiled. Khuna was good at his job. The two men would be assisted from the Hanging Monkey with very explicit instructions not to return. Ever. There were a couple of shouts from the entrance and then the sound of hard flesh pounding on flesh, then double thuds. Khuna walked back into the room and returned to Corky.

"Doc Galloway is going to be busy," Khuna said.

"How busy?" Corky looked at his bouncer.

"They both have broken arms. Discourages fighting," Khuna grinned.

"That it does," Corky agreed.

Nick Fortune had showered and shaved and dressed in a clean white shirt and khaki trousers and brown boots. Walking back to town in the dark was dicey at best. There were a lot of venomous creatures on Motugra, from snakes and centipedes to spiders and scorpions. There were other larger predators, as well, which was why his gun was holstered under his tropical weight jacket.

Nick lit a Lucky Strike as he walked along the path. The moon was rising in a midnight blue sky, bathing the path in silver and jet. Something crashed in the bush and Fortune eyed the shadows warily. He thought about Burke. The man made him twitchy. There was a reason for it. The lights of town grew brighter and soon he was out of the jungle and on the dirt streets. The air was cool tonight but not uncomfortably so after the heat of the day. The night was clear and a faint breeze was blowing in off the ocean. Tiki torches were burning in front of the monkey and Nick could see the monkey sitting on a branch watching all who entered and left. He made a gun of his fist and extended forefinger and shot the monkey with it. The monkey grinned and chattered at him as he walked through the batwing doors.

Corky was on the piano playing a jazzy rendition of "As Time Goes By." Jimmy Dolan was at a corner table and Miko was behind the bar. Khuna moved silently around the room, going where it looked like trouble might break out and stifling it by his mere presence. Nick walked over to Dolan's table and dropped into a chair across from his fellow American. A waitress came to the table with a mug of beer and placed it in front of him.

Nick took a sip and sighed appreciatively.

"Rough day, Nick?" Jimmy asked.

"I've had better. Met a friend of yours today, a guy named Burke. Claims to be an archeologist," Fortune replied.

"How did you meet Burke? And no, he's not a friend but he paid in cash. I figured the cannibals on Papogo would make short work of him," Dolan replied, slurping at his own beer. Nick wondered how many his friend had drank so far.

"He came running out of the jungle with the natives on his tail and jumped on the boat as I pulled away from the dock. He cost me further supply runs, bucko," Nick said, his tone cold and hard as diamonds.

"Sorry, Pal. I had no way of knowing he was gonna rile up the natives," Jimmy shrugged, sipping his own drink.

"Jimmy," Nick looked at him.

"Okay, I got it, Nick, I owe you," Jimmy shook his head.

"It cost me a contract, Jimmy. A big one," Nick told him.

"I'm really sorry about that, Nick. I'll front you the amount for the next three months," Jimmy said.

"Glad to hear you say that, Jimmy. A thousand a month is good wages," Nick smiled.

"A thousand a month!" Jimmy sputtered.

"That's what it cost me," Nick glared at him.

Grace Thomas felt almost numb. She couldn't believe what she had read. There is no way that Nick Fortune was a cold-blooded killer. She hadn't known him long, but she knew him well enough to know the kind of man he was. Former mobster, maybe; killer, no.

She needed to talk to Nick, she needed to speak to him face to face. She needed to see the truth in his eyes. Grace took a deep breath and let it out and then headed out the door for the Hanging Monkey. She would cable her editor in the morning and have him ship her everything that the newspaper had on the murders of Joan Mulgrew and Dane Carter. She would get to the bottom of it and clear Nick's name once and for all!

Nellie Jonas was at the microphone and Kapelli, one of the natives, was playing the piano and doing a pretty serviceable job of it. Nick was on his third beer and not looking happy. He wondered if he had done the right thing by having Mortimer deliver those cables. Maybe it would have been better to have burned them instead and let her never know the truth.

"You could never do that Nick. You're not the kind of man who could ever lie to a woman you love," Joanie's voice filled his head. Nick closed his eyes and he could see her face.

"You know me better than I know myself, Joanie," Nick whispered.

"That's right, Nick. I know you loved me, but I'm gone. You have feelings for her. Let her know, Nick. Don't hang on to me when the real thing is right there in front of you," Joanie's voice said.

"Right," Nick nodded. He opened his eye. The music and song were still going on, and no one had noticed him talking to himself. Nick sighed, knowing he had been lucky. Closing his eyes had been an unfortunate choice given where he was. Nick had enemies and it appeared that they were closing in on him.

Burke had cleaned up and was headed back into to town. Richter was supposed to meet him at the Hanging Monkey. He would exchange the jewel for the money there. And then with luck, he could take care of both Dolan and Fortune and get off this Godforsaken island.

Burke headed through the darkness towards the Hanging Monkey. He had the Eye of Ka wrapped in a soft cloth in his pocket. He would wait on Richter; the Nazi had a habit of being late.

He and Richter had never been friends, but the Nazi paid well and that was what mattered the most to Burke. He liked cash and the Nazi always seemed to have plenty of it. Burke had purchased a bottle earlier and had worked his way through most of it before heading for the Hanging Monkey.

His gait was unsteady as he made his way from the hotel to the drinking establishment that Richter had named as a meeting point after he had retrieved the jewel. His gun was holstered on his hip, but Burke hadn't bothered to unfasten the safety strap. There were noises from the surrounding jungle, but he paid them no mind. He feared nothing that stalked the night. Burke took a hit from the bottle clenched in his fist and tilted his head back. He stepped out onto the boardwalk and made his way to the Hanging Monkey. He was just steps from the door when he heard a whooshing sound, and something struck him in the chest, delivering a blinding pain.

Burke looked down and was amazed to see the hilt of a knife sticking from his chest. "Bloody hell…" he gasped before tumbling to the boardwalk, a crimson stain spreading across his chest.

Grace Thomas was making her way to the Hanging Monkey when she noticed something out of the ordinary. A man was crumpled on the boardwalk. She walked up to him, thinking at first he was a drunk that had staggered outside before passing out. It was only as she drew closer that she noticed the red puddle spreading around him. Grace screamed, loudly and shrilly, the sound cutting through the night like an air-raid siren! It even cut through the din inside the Hanging Monkey.

Nick Fortune was immediately on his feet and charging out the door, his automatic in his fist. He skidded to a stop as he recognized Grace and the dead man at her feet. Grace looked at him with a mixture of fear and relief in her eyes. Nick called over his shoulder. "Get the Magistrate of Justice!"

"Oh Nick, I just found him," Grace sobbed as the Italian American holstered his pistol and took her in his arms.

"How terrible for you," Nick said softly, consoling her. He didn't tell her that he knew the man, that Burke had been on his boat earlier during the day, for he knew that would only make her suspicious of him, even more so than she already had to be after reading those cables!

"Nick, I must talk to you!" Grace looked urgently up into his eyes.

"Now is not the time, Dear," Nick whispered back, hugging her tightly to him.

"But Nick…" Grace started. Fortune cut her off.

"I mean it, Grace. Right now we have a killer to find and a murder to solve," Fortune gestured at the dead man on the boardwalk. In the trees the monkey chattered angrily at them. Fortune briefly wished the animal could talk, for it had certainly seen the killer.

"Khuna, run and get the magistrate, see if Colonel Smythe is on the island as well," Corky O'Brian commanded.

"Any idea who it is?" Jimmy Dolan asked, still holding a beer mug in his hand.

"Yeah," Nick had rolled the body over to see the man's face. "It's your buddy that caught a ride back here on my boat today."

"Holy cow!" Dolan exclaimed.

※ ※ ※

"Now this is shaping up to be a fine mess," Corky shook his head as he listened to Jimmy and Nick.

"That it is, my friend," Nick replied. There were too many ears at the moment to relate the story to Corky of how he and Jimmy both knew the dead man.

"Anything either one of you needs to tell before the colonel gets here?" Corky looked at them both.

"Nope," Nick replied, he still held his gun, his eyes scanning the jungle, searching for some sign that the killer was nearby and watching.

"Not me," Dolan took another swig of beer from his mug.

"I hope you're both being honest with me," Corky scowled.

"I hope they are as well," Grace said, looking at each of the three men carefully.

"What Ho! What's going on here?" Colonel Neville Smythe asked as he rounded the corner and saw the body. Khuna was at his side.

"We have a dead man," Nick Fortune lit a Lucky Strike.

"I can see that, Mr. Fortune," Colonel Smythe replied drily.

"Glad to hear it." Nick grinned. It was his own way of dealing with his own precarious situation.

"Anybody know him?" Smythe looked at them all.

"He said his name was Burke and he claimed to be an archeologist," Nick explained.

"And you doubt that?" Smythe asked, looking him in the eye.

"I have no reason to. Picked him up on an island trading post and brought him back here," Nick shrugged.

"I dropped him off there a couple of days ago," Jimmy added, taking another swig of beer.

"Either of you know why he was killed?" Smythe looked them both over.

"No," Nick replied.

"Me either," Jimmy added.

"That being cleared, Colonel, we'll be leaving the rest for you to figure out," Corky announced. The rest of them headed back to the Hanging Monkey in a group, leaving Smythe there to wonder about the dead man.

Two strangers were inside the Hanging Monkey when Nick and the others returned. One was a tall pale oriental in long flowing green robes with golden dragons embroidered on them with golden thread. A pillbox cap adorned his head. A long thin mustache covered his face and hung down below his chin. His eyes were like glittering emeralds. The other man was a large muscular Chinese with a flat nose and dark almond-shaped eyes. Of the two, Nick Fortune decided the thinner, paler man in the green robes was the more dangerous.

"Who the bloody hell are you?" Corky asked, knowing everyone else in the bar.

"My name is Chi Pei and I am here to collect something from a man that had recovered some of my property," the taller man replied.

"And the bleeding sod behind you?" Corky demanded.

"My servant, Chang," Chi Pei replied.

"Who were you meeting?" Nick Fortune demanded.

"His name was Burke," Chi Pei replied dismissively.

"You're a bit late then. He's dead," Nick replied, his cold blue eye never leaving Chi Pei's face.

"That is most unfortunate," Chi Pei shrugged.

"Most certainly," Nick nodded.

"Nobody leaves until my men have questioned you," Colonel Neville

Smythe announced as he entered the bar. He looked at Chi Pei.

"And who might you be?"

"My name is Chi Pei," the Chinaman replied.

"You know the dead man?" Smythe asked, raising an eyebrow.

"By reputation only," Chi Pei shrugged.

"I'll want to speak to you at length in the morning," Smythe told him.

"I am your obedient servant," Chi Pei replied, bowing slightly.

"Certainly," Colonel Smythe nodded, and then he looked at Nick. "Who found the body?"

"That would be me, Colonel," Grace stepped forward.

"You are?" the colonel asked.

"Grace Thomas, foreign correspondent for the New York Clarion," Grace replied.

It took more than two hours for Smythe to complete his questioning. The body had been removed from the boardwalk and taken to the local undertaker for him to do an autopsy. Finally, Smythe dismissed everyone and ordered the Hanging Monkey closed for the night. Nick Fortune caught up with Grace Thomas and offered to walk her home.

He wanted to search Burke's room but figured the colonel already had done so. Grace clutched his arm tightly as they walked back to her hotel. They stopped in front of her door. Nick looked at her, her face and hair like alabaster in the moonlight. "You said you wanted to ask me something," Nick gazed into her dark blue eyes.

"I cabled New York about you, Nick. I shouldn't have done so. The F.B.I. is sending an agent to question you or perhaps even arrest you and take you back to New York," tears streamed down her cheeks.

"I know," Nick replied softly, almost sighing.

"Nick, I didn't mean to cause you trouble, you must believe me," Grace looked into his eye.

"I know, Grace. My past was bound to catch up to me sooner or later," Nick folded her into his arms and kissed her gently.

"Did you kill that woman?" Grace asked after the kiss was broken.

"No, but I did kill the man that murdered her," Nick replied honestly.

"Thank God! I'll do what I can to help you, Nick. No matter what!" Grace smiled at him through her tears. It struck him that Grace actually felt the same way about him that he did about her!

"I love you Grace, but until I can clear my name…" Nick let his sentence hang.

"I'll help you with that, Nick, no matter what it takes!" Grace replied and he kissed her again. This time Nick broke the kiss and pointed at the door.

"Get some sleep, we'll figure out what to do in the morning," Nick smiled.

"Yes, yes we will," Grace smiled, her face lighting up. Nick waited until she was inside and her door was closed and locked before starting to his own bungalow.

Danger walked in darkness. Nick Fortune could sense it as he walked the shadowed path to his bungalow. Even without the murder on the boardwalk outside the Hanging Monkey, he did not trust the Chinese gentleman who had appeared in the bar looking for Burke. There was something inherently evil about the Chinaman. Nick didn't trust him.

Jimmy Dolan had gone to his room at the residential hotel where he lived. He had noticed that Nick had walked Grace home. It made him smile. Nick needed someone to take care of him. He had been a lone wolf for as long as Jimmy had known him. He was concerned about Burke's murder. He was also somewhat creeped out by the appearance of the Chinaman who claimed Burke was working for him.

There was something unnerving about the Chinaman and the mute giant that accompanied him as a bodyguard. Jimmy flipped on the lights as he entered his room, his revolver in his fist. Seeing that it was empty, he breathed a sigh of relief. He holstered his revolver and shrugged out of his brown leather bomber jacket. He tossed it onto a hook on the wall and locked the door behind him.

Jimmy walked to his bed and sat down, kicking his boots off. He opened a drawer in the nightstand next to the bed and drew out a bottle of whiskey. There was a shot glass in the drawer and he removed it as well. Jimmy twisted off the cap and poured himself a shot. Jimmy pulled out his gun and laid it on the nightstand beside him as he sipped the whiskey. Before long he had fallen back on the bed, sound asleep.

"He entered the room…revolver in his fist."

Corky O'Brian walked through the bar, making sure all the doors were locked. Things were getting strange fast and he didn't like it. Didn't like it a bit. First there had been the murder and then the sudden appearance of the Chinaman inside the bar. There was more going on than met the eye.

No, something was afoot. Something that none of them knew about. Corky planned to do some investigating of his own. Smythe wouldn't like it, but Corky didn't really care what the colonel thought.

Chi Pei returned to the Chinese junk that had carried him to Motugra. The murder of Burke was an unwanted complication. The archeologist had admitted that there were others interested in the jewel known as the Eye of Ka. For the moment he wondered who they might be.

Chang would find out. The dacoit was excellent at eliciting information from those who opposed Chi Pei. The Devil Doctor smiled at the thought. Even now the dacoit was searching for answers in the darkness. Chi Pei smiled as he fired his opium pipe.

Corky O'Brian had found where Burke had been staying and had gone to see what he could find out. A search of the dead man's room might reveal why he was murdered. Corky approached the door and noticed it was already partially open. He drew a Webley .45 revolver from his waistband and held it at the ready as he approached the open door.

His palm was sweating on the wooden grip, and the checkering was biting into his flesh. Corky threw the door open, the revolver leveled at his waist. "Stay where you are!" Corky commanded, thumbing the hammer of the revolver back.

Nick fortune stood there, Jimmy Dolan at his side. Both men held guns. Corky grinned. Nick holstered his gun and smiled at Corky. "Fancy meeting you here," Nick quipped.

"I should have known. Neither of you was likely to let this go," Corky shook his head.

"Nope, Burke was carrying something worth killing him for. Figured it might be a good idea to find out what it was," Nick replied.

"Besides, Smythe won't come here until morning. He enjoys his routine too much," Dolan shrugged.

"Let's be hoping you are right about that," Corky nodded.

"Close the door and help us hunt. He was leaving Papogo in an awful hurry and had riled up the natives. There had to be a reason for that," Nick said.

"He said something when I dropped him off about a rare jewel," Jimmy's brow wrinkled as he thought hard about his first meeting with the now deceased archeologist.

"He said he had been in a temple and it made the natives angry," Nick added.

"Which indicates he had stolen something of great value to them," Corky said.

"This is turning into a real mess," Nick summed it up.

"That it is, old friend, that it is," Corky replied.

"So where in this dump would you hide a jewel if you didn't have it on you?" Jimmy asked.

"How do you know he didn't have it on him?" Corky looked at the pilot.

"I checked," Jimmy shrugged.

"Laddie," the Irishman shook his head.

"Can we discuss this later? Like after we find the jewel?" Nick asked.

"I believe that would be a very good idea," Corky agreed.

"So what are we going to do with it if we do find it?" Jimmy asked.

"We return it to Papogo," Nick cut in immediately.

"But..." Jimmy started.

"No buts, Jimmy. It belongs to the people living on Papogo," Nick's tone brooked no nonsense.

"You sure know how to kill a good time," Jimmy grumbled.

"Tell that to Burke," Corky added.

Chang froze in the shadows outside the hotel. His master had not considered that others might be searching for the prized jewel known as the Eye of Ka. Just from listening the dacoit realized that the three men in the room would be formidable fighters. Even he might not be able to take them all. Chang had spent many years in service to Chi Pei, known by his enemies as the Devil Doctor. Failing to acquire the jewel was not an option. Chang would wait quietly in the shadows until the three men had left, then he would conduct his own search.

Klaus Richter had faded quietly back to the shadows after the body of the archeologist had been discovered. He had fronted Burke a lot of money to locate a mystical jewel known as the Eye of Ka. It was rumored to reside in a lost temple somewhere in the Motugra Island chain. *Der Führer* wanted the jewel. It was Richter's job to find it.

Klaus had been held up by a communiqué from Berlin; it had required an immediate report on the situation. Of course afterwards he had been forced to send word that the previous message has caused him to miss the rendezvous and that the man he was meeting had been assassinated.

Rather than go search the dead man's room, he had elected to go to the coroner's office to view the body. Richter had stayed in the shadows approaching the building that doubled as hospital and morgue. Silas Montague, who was both doctor and coroner, had locked the doors and gone home for the night. So far as Richter was concerned, that was a good thing in that it would allow him to examine the body and make sure that Burke had not been carrying the jewel on him when he died.

Richter quickly picked the lock and entered the building. He wanted to leave no trace of his presence around the body. It took a few moments for him to find it. The knife was still protruding from the dead man's chest. Richter reached out with a gloved fist and tugged on the knife, drawing it partially from the wound. The blade wasn't straight. It was curved. A Kris. Richter frowned. The Kris originated in Persia, from there it had found its way to the Orient. The question now was who had killed Burke and why? Had they been after the jewel? Or was it something else? Something in the man's past?

Richter slipped back outside, relocking the door of the morgue behind him. He had a lot of thinking to do. He knew that there were others interested in the jewel, and they were every bit as deadly. Chi Pei was well-known to the Nazi hierarchy and Richter had his own suspicions where the Devil Doctor was concerned. He needed to find out who on the island had been in contact with Burke.

Grace Thomas lay on her bed. She had spent a good deal of time weeping over what she had done to Nick Fortune by bringing the authorities down on him. The look in his eyes had hurt her, hurt her to the core of her being, when she had told him the F.B.I. was sending an agent out to question him.

Nick was troubled; she had no doubt of that. Now he was facing even worse trouble, and it was all her fault. She had to find a way to help him. She sat up; there might be a way! She would take all the information about Burke and cable the Clarion, see what the paper had on him. She might be able to trade Burke for Nick. It was a good plan.

Klaus Richter moved through the darkness. He had known that his time was limited once the body had been found. He had thought about going immediately to the dead man's room but had held off. Even he didn't know who had arranged Burke's murder, and it was something that he was desperate to find out!

The German spy ran his fingers through his close-cropped blonde hair. The night air was cooler, but not cool enough to keep him from sweating. The moon was high in the sky, painting the jungle in silver and jet. The town had grown quiet with only the animal sounds from the jungle filling the night, along with the waves crashing on the beach with the incoming tide.

His trip to the morgue had given him some information. The man had been killed with a Persian-style blade that had made its way to the Orient. The stone was not on Burke's body. So where was it? In Burke's room? He headed for the hotel.

He moved through the shadows towards the building where Burke had been staying. Richter waited in the shadows as he watched three men leave the dead man's hotel room. Richter crept forward. He kept to the shadows as much as possible until he reached the door. It was locked. He had expected no less.

Richter removed a set of lockpicks from his pocket and went to work on the lock. It took less than a minute for him to get it open and step inside. Richter eased the door shut behind him and moved deeper into the room. He never noticed the doorknob turning and the door opening behind him.

"What do you think happened?" Corky O'Brian asked as he poured whiskey into three shot glasses inside the Hanging Monkey.

"I think Burke had lined up several buyers for whatever it was he stole. One of them didn't want to pay what Burke wanted for it. So they decided to take it before the other interested parties," Nick Fortune sipped at his shot of whiskey.

"Or maybe he just was unlucky and got mugged," Jimmy Dolan shrugged.

"If that be the case I'll be sending a cable to get the odds," Corky snorted.

"It could happen, you know there are a lot of unsavory types passing through here," Jimmy looked slightly hurt.

"And we are looking at one of the worst," Nick grinned.

"Ah shucks, Nick," Jimmy laughed.

"Nick is right, Jimmy, there is danger about the island and it all comes back to whatever Burke stole. We figure out what it was, and perhaps we can put a stop to this," Corky drained his glass. "You boys want to crash here for the night?"

"I have to wonder if that might not be the safer option," Nick shrugged and Jimmy nodded his head.

They awoke to a lot of shouting from the street. Nick sat up and rubbed his eyes as Corky made his way to the front doors and unlocked them, stepping out into the morning sunshine to see what was going on. Jimmy was still leaning on the table snoring loudly. Nick reached over and kicked his chair, bringing Dolan up swinging at no one. When Dolan's eyes focused on Nick, the boat captain nodded towards the doors. They stepped outside to see Grace Thomas hurrying up the street towards them.

"Grace, what's happened?" Nick met her at the end of the boardwalk.

"They found a dead man in Burke's room. He was apparently murdered there last night," Grace sobbed. Nick shot a look over his shoulder at Corky and Dolan. There had been no body when they had searched the room. Whomever it was had to have gone in later.

"Do you know who it was?" Fortune asked.

"A German, Colonel Smythe said. I didn't catch his name," Grace looked up at him. "What's going on, Nick?"

"That is what we are trying to find out," Nick replied honestly. He didn't like things like this happening. It was too much like New York!

"Come in and get something to steady you, lass. It's a bit early but, under the circumstances, no one will mind," Corky told her as Nick ushered her into the Hanging Monkey.

"Corky, does Khuna have any contacts on Papogo?" Nick asked.

"Khuna has fought all over the Motugra chain. He can find out anything," Corky replied.

"When he shows up, get him on it," Nick commanded.

"Who'll act as bouncer while Khuna is gone? This place can get pretty rough," Grace observed.

"Jimmy and me will be hanging around a few days. Between us and Corky and Miko, we should be able to handle it," Fortune replied.

"Miko disappeared last night when that Chinaman showed up," Grace noted.

"I kinda wondered about that, too," Jimmy scratched his chin.

"I'll ask her about that," Corky nodded.

"But do you think she'll give you an answer?" Grace looked at him.

"She will," Corky replied grimly.

Colonel Neville Smythe looked around the room. Two murders in less than twenty-four hours. It was bloody aggravating! He had never had this much trouble in the islands. The presence of the Chinese junk in the harbor did little to ease his mind. He had heard too many rumors about the Chinese gentleman known as Doctor Chi Pei. In his home country his name was spoken of with a mixture of awe and fear. Whispers of depraved experiments had reached the British regiments stationed there. For him to be here on Motugra, with all this happening, well it had to be more than just coincidence!

Also the way that the German, Richter, had been killed! He had been strangled in the fashion of the dacoits, and Chi Pei had been accompanied by such a man the night before. Then there was the cable he had received about an American Federal Agent on his way to Motugra to question Nick Fortune. Of the men that hung out at the Hanging Monkey, Fortune caused the least trouble of them all.

And then there was that fool of a banker complaining about the chimp that kept watch outside the Hanging Monkey. For his part, Smythe would rather do something about the tight-fisted banker than the jungle creature. He would speak to O'Brian and see if there was anything that the bar owner might be able to do about the beast.

Smythe pulled out his watch. It was time for him to head for the coroner's inquest on the man murdered the night before. He would then head over to the Hanging Monkey and see what he could find out there.

Miko looked up at the man she called master, thrilled that he remembered her. He had given her a signal when he had entered the bar the night before, and she had gone straight to his Junk to await his pleasure. It was a night she would never forget. "Your instructions, O Celestial One?" she asked.

"I want the Eye of Ka. The American had it on him when he left his room, but it was no longer present when his body was found. We must discover who has it," Chi Pei replied, stroking her silken hair.

"I will keep my ears open, master and report at the earliest opportunity," Miko replied.

"Do that. I fear I will be tied up for a large portion of the day with the local authorities. They will try to discover if I had any part in what happened to the American," Chi Pei replied.

"As you command, O Celestial One," Miko bowed and left the room. Chi Pei leaned back into the Emerald Throne, forming a pyramid of his fingers as he contemplated his next move.

Jake Sloan wandered into the Hanging Monkey a little after the excitement had abated. He walked over and dropped into a chair next to Jimmy Dolan. "Wild night, boss?" the mechanic that kept the Goose flying asked. A waitress brought him a cup of coffee. Another native was working a grill behind the bar, making bacon and eggs for everyone.

"What makes you think that, lad," Corky asked from across the table.

"Well, there were plenty of folks roaming around during the wee hours. One of them even tried to mess with the Goose but, after I nearly dinged their head with an open end wrench, they left in a big hurry," Jake shrugged.

"Who would want to be messing around with the Goose?" Jimmy wondered aloud.

"Who have you pissed off besides me?" Nick looked at him disapprovingly.

"I've been gone a few days so there couldn't be too many," Jimmy scratched his head.

"What about those two gentlemen you two fought with yesterday?" Grace eyed Dolan and Corky.

"Khuna broke their arms when they came back. They would likely still be at the Doc's place," Corky shook his head, a stray lock of red hair tumbling down to hang like a comma above his right eye.

"Grace, tell us about when you found the body," Nick said suddenly, his expression intense.

"I was coming to see you. I had just started up the boardwalk when I heard an awful racket, and I saw the man on the boardwalk. At first I thought he had just passed out and then I saw the blood. At that point I screamed, and you fellows know the rest," she put her face in her hands.

"Gracie, this is important. That awful racket, was it coming from inside or outside," Nick asked.

"I'm not sure, Nick. I just don't know," Grace shook her head.

"What is it, Nick?" Corky watched him carefully. The Irishman had come to know the Italian American well in his time on the island. Fortune was coming up with an idea.

"I'm not sure, Corky. A hunch maybe, but nothing that I can prove or even voice yet. Let me think about it a little longer," Nick said as he dug out his pack of Lucky Strikes and shook one free and fired it up. He exhaled a cloud of smoke that was dispelled by the slowly turning ceiling fans.

"So what do we do now?" Grace asked.

"We wait and see what turns up," Nick replied.

"Where's Khuna?" Grace asked, noticing that the squat Motugran bouncer was nowhere to be seen.

"Trying to find some answers," Corky smiled secretively.

"I need to go over to the cable office," Grace stood, looking more confident than she had when she had first arrived.

"I'll walk you over," Nick stood as well. He looked at Corky and Dolan. "Back in a little while."

Together he and Grace Thomas walked out the batwings. Jake Sloan shook his head as he dug into a plate of scrambled eggs and bacon. "You guys are all nuts," Sloan mumbled through his food.

"No argument there," Jimmy laughed.

Nick Fortune dropped Grace Thomas off at the cable office and he headed for the dock. After Jake's comment about someone trying to board the Goose he wanted to check Fortune's Folly. There was no one to watch over it, as there was the Goose. He had a deep suspicion about Burke's murder and a possible witness that no one had considered: the witness who might indeed hold the final clue to Burke's murder!

Nick had flicked away a cigarette that was nearly burned out and had fired up another one. Burke had rubbed him the wrong way from the moment that they had met.

Nick had never liked the alleged archeologist from the start. The man had struck him as a thief from the word go. That he had stolen something from the people of Papogo was neither a surprise nor a shock.

He wanted to know more about the so-called archeologist and what he had been after.

Grace Thomas was back in the bar but Nick Fortune had yet to return. It was now later afternoon and neither Corky nor Dolan had seen Nick either. Grace was beginning to get worried about the man she was falling in love with. Just then she heard a loud commotion out front and turned to face the door. Poke Doohan stormed through the batwings, without his beat up Derby. "O'Brian!" the banker shouted angrily.

"What's the problem, Poke?" Corky asked, walking out of the office looking annoyed.

"That damn beastie out front! It stole my brand new hat again!" Poke Doohan roared.

"Then maybe you should take it to yon haberdashery," O'Brian shook his head.

"I hold you responsible for the beast because you keep it around!" Doohan roared back.

"I don't 'keep' the monkey around, Poke. It comes and goes as it pleases. The Monkey was here when I built the place," O'Brian retorted.

"And you let it stay!" Doohan roared again. Corky O'Brian strode across the bar and slammed a hard-knuckled fist hard into Poke Doohan's chin, sending the Scottish banker wind-milling backwards towards the door. O'Brian followed, hitting the banker in the gut and doubling him over. A third blow sent him backwards through the batwings and crashing onto the boardwalk outside. The Monkey was sitting in the branches screeching and chattering. It threw a new felt brown derby at Doohan.

Brown liquid splashed out across the Scotsman's face.

"I share his opinion, Doohan. Don't come back here for at least a week. You won't be welcome," Corky said grimly, then he turned and stepped back inside the bar.

"What was that all about?" Grace asked as Corky walked back to the bar. Miko sat a bottle of beer in front of her boss.

"Poke Doohan has hated our little mascot from the first day I opened the place, and the monkey pretty much feels the same way about him," Corky took a long pull at the bottle.

"What was all that noise before Doohan came in, and then again when he went out?" Grace asked.

"That was the Chimp. He raises an awful ruckus anytime Doohan comes around," Corky replied.

"Really?" Grace asked, a thoughtful expression on her face.

"Every time that tight-fisted banker shows his face the Monkey has a fit," Corky said.

"Does it ever act that way with anyone else?" Grace asked, her expression intense.

"Only Omar Selim," Corky replied.

"Who is Omar?" Grace asked.

"Omar is a Persian that has a small rug shop near the center of town. He and Doohan are pretty tight," Corky replied.

"I see. Corky, I need to go to the cable office once more. If Nick comes in, ask him to wait for me," Grace said.

"Of course," Corky agreed. Grace flashed him a smile as she slid off her stool and headed out the door. She wanted a look at Omar for herself.

The air was hot and humid and her blouse was sticking to her as she stepped out into it. A germ of an idea had started to form and she wanted to test it to see if it would grow.

"I thank you, Mr. Fortune, for attending the interrogation of Chi Pei with me. He has a fearsome and dangerous reputation in this part of the world," Colonel Smythe said.

"Not a problem, Colonel." Nick Fortune replied, lighting up a Lucky Strike. Nick exhaled a cloud of smoke as he thought about the time they had spent talking to the man known throughout the Orient as the Devil Doctor.

"Something is going on, Colonel. I'm not sure yet what it is, but I know it has something to do with whatever Burke took from Papogo Island. Chi Pei is an interested party, as was the German found in Burke's room. What we need to discover is what was taken," Nick decided.

"Splendid idea, Mr. Fortune. Can you offer any suggestions?" Colonel Smythe looked at him as he fired a pipe. The English officer blew smoke rings into the air.

"It threw a new...derby at Doohan."

"I wish I could, Colonel. I don't think Chi Pei had anything to do with Burke's death. His junk didn't even arrive in the harbor until it had happened. Granted he showed up quick, but it was after Burke had been killed. Now for the German, he looks like a good candidate for that one," Fortune replied, blowing a few smoke rings of his own.

"His dacoit, you mean," Smythe said.

"Pretty much," Nick agreed.

"He seems a fairly obvious choice, given the cause of death," Smythe replied.

"He does," Nick agreed.

"Which brings us back to Burke," Smythe said.

"It does," Nick agreed

"So what do you think?" Smythe asked.

"I think that Burke stole something very important and that he had buyers lined up for it. I also think that whatever it was needs to be returned to the people of Papogo," Nick replied.

"I agree with you, lad. However, first we need to find it," Smythe nodded.

"I have a suspicion about that, but it may take a day or two to prove out," Nick announced.

"Contact me when you are sure. I am holding up the travel permits for the F.B.I. man that is coming. He wants to talk to you in a bad way; however, His Majesty's Service feels you may prove invaluable to us right now," Smythe told him.

Nick nodded and headed out of the office. He had wanted to be in on the questioning of Chi Pei, though he was fairly certain that the Chinaman had nothing to do with Burke's murder. He had much to consider as he headed back towards the Hanging Monkey.

Grace Thomas sipped iced tea as she kept an eye on the shop of Omar Selim. The Persian rarely appeared outside his shop so she had yet to get a good look at him. A theory was starting to form based on the facts, but she needed to see Omar Selim before she could say for sure.

She had been thinking a lot about when she had come upon the body the night before. There had been more than the loud noise, noise which she now believed to have been made by the monkey that watched people go in and out of the bar. For something—or someone—had darted into the shadows at the edge of her vision. It had happened so fast that she had barely realized she had seen anything and had in fact dismissed it as imagination until Nick had made her think about it.

The monkey's reaction to Doohan had started her thinking. That was why she had asked Corky if there was anyone else to whom the monkey reacted like that. Movement near the shop caught her attention and she realized it was the two Chinese men that had appeared mysteriously in the Hanging Monkey right after the murder. What business, Grace wondered, would they have with Omar Selim? Because they certainly didn't look the type to be interested in Persian rugs.

Chi Pei almost seemed to glide as he entered the shop of Omar Selim. The Persian had been a source of useful information in the past and he hoped that the man would be this time. Omar operated on what some would call the seamier side of things, and he was none to particular about whom he purchased his wares from, nor to whom he sold them.

Omar was a man motivated by greed. Chi Pei had often made it worth the Persian's while to provide him with information that Chi Pei had wanted. He was hopeful that on this occasion Omar would know the current whereabouts of the Eye of Ka.

Chi Pei's interest in the stone came solely from the power it would give him over the denizens of these South Sea Islands, and perhaps a remote base to work from if things became too difficult in China. Between the fear in the current government and the Japanese incursions, the political climate was growing a bit too volatile for his taste. He had bases established all over the world, but none quite reflected the beauty of the islands.

"Welcome to my humble rug shop," Omar Selim said as he stepped out from behind a beaded curtain. It took a moment for him to recognize his customer. "Celestial Master! What brings you to my humble abode?" Omar asked.

"I come seeking knowledge, old friend, knowledge that I believe you may possess," Chi Pei replied in the Persian's native tongue.

"I will do my best to find the information you require," Omar replied.

"There is a jewel known as the Eye of Ka. It is said to reside within these islands. The American Burke was said to have recovered it before his untimely death, at the hand of a Persian blade," Chi Pei's emerald eyes never left him as the words were spoken.

"I have heard rumors, but I have not seen such a jewel," Omar stammered.

"Are you sure?" Chi Pei's eyes seemed to grow larger, encompassing everything.

"I know Burke," Omar said dully. "He offered me the jewel, but at a price that was far too exorbitant for this humble merchant," Omar admitted.

"Who else was Burke dealing with?" Chi Pei asked.

"There was a German, a man named Richter. We were in a bidding war," Omar said.

"So if the German has not gotten the jewel, and you don't have the jewel, who does?" Chi Pei asked.

"I don't know," Omar replied.

"You are very fortunate, old friend, because I believe you," Chi Pei smiled.

"And if you did not?" Omar asked.

"You would be dead," Chi Pei replied, smiling. The tall Oriental turned and headed for the door. Omar watched him go and dropped to his knees, sending prayers to Allah. He knew he had just barely escaped going to meet his god.

Grace Thomas watched as Chi Pei and his man Chang exited from the rug shop. She felt that the Chinaman moved with a relaxed posture that had not been present when he had first entered the place. The dacoit moved with him like a shadow as they headed for the dock.

It was time, Grace decided, to return to the Hanging Monkey to see what the others had discovered. She emptied her glass of iced tea and headed across the town towards the bar.

Corky O'Brian was drinking a shot of Irish Whiskey when Grace Thomas stepped through the batwings of the Hanging Monkey. "Have you seen Nick?" Grace asked.

"Not yet, but he should be along soon," Corky replied.

"I think I may know what this is all about," Grace smiled.

"Nick will be glad to know that," Corky replied.

"This is getting pretty creepy if you ask me," Jimmy Dolan said after swallowing a large gulp of beer. He paused for a second to wipe the foam from his mouth on his sleeve. It was getting dark and the bar was starting to fill up with the evening crowd. The new kid on the piano had talent and was playing some lively tunes. Some of the patrons were raising their voices and joining in.

"You're calling a good night fer me establishment creepy?" Corky scowled at the pilot.

"Not this, the whole murder thing. We don't normally have unsolved murders on Motugra," Jimmy muttered.

"Well it's not like it isn't being investigated, by the authorities as well as ourselves," Corky reminded him. Miko had moved down the bar closer to them and Jimmy signaled for another beer. The Chinese bartender nodded and pulled a fresh mug from under the bar and filled it from a tapped keg and carried it down to Dolan.

"Have you heard anything from Nick or Khuna?" Jimmy asked.

"I haven't, and 'tis starting to worry me," Corky admitted with a heavy sigh. At that moment, Nick Fortune walked through the batwing doors, Colonel Smythe at his heels. Nick looked around a moment before heading across the bar to them.

"Have you seen Grace?" Nick asked, his expression one of concern.

"She was in earlier looking for you. She said she might have this mess all figured out. Then she headed back to the hotel," Corky replied.

"I was afraid of this. We were just at the hotel and Grace wasn't there," Nick said soberly.

"We'll join the search," Corky stood up, Dolan right behind him. Just then the bar fell silent and Khuna had stepped inside, followed by some of the fiercest looking men that Corky had ever seen. It took him no time at all to realize that they were cannibals from Papogo Island.

"I know what was stolen, and these gents behind me want it back," Khuna pointed over his shoulder with his thumb. Even Colonel Smythe didn't know what to make of the frightening band of warriors. One of the men tapped Khuna's shoulder and pointed at Nick. "He says you helped the man escape that stole the Eye of Ka," Khuna said, giving Fortune a hard look.

"Burke jumped on my boat, but I didn't know he had stolen anything, and those fellas didn't look like they really wanted to talk about what he did. They looked more interested in putting us both in a cooking pot," Nick replied. Khuna almost smiled.

"Probably a good bet," the Motugran warrior replied.

"You think?" Nick shook his head as he pulled out a Lucky Strike and fired it up. "So what exactly is the Eye of Ka?" Nick was worried about Grace but he also was curious about whatever Burke had stolen from Papogo Island.

"The Eye of Ka is a gemstone that adorned a statue of one of their gods. The temple was located deep in the jungle. No way to know how Burke found out about it, but he stole the stone and they want it back in a very bad way," Khuna replied.

"And I think I might know how to get it for them, Khuna. But I need an hour, and we need to find Grace," Nick replied.

Grace Thomas was in serious trouble and she knew it. She had watched as the Chinamen had left and Omar had hurriedly closed up shop. She had followed him to a small house on the outskirts of town and then made a trip to the Hanging Monkey to look for Nick, but she found that he hadn't been there. Then she had made what might have been a fatal error. She had gone back to the house to which she had tailed the Persian.

She had slipped inside, and then somebody had slugged her from behind and tied her up and gagged her. Not that screaming would have summoned any help, not with the house situated so far on the outskirts of town.

Her head hurt from where she had been knocked out. The question was how could she get loose? The room was nearly pitch black, so she was fairly certain that it was dark outside. She hoped that Nick and the others would be looking for her. Grace decided to roll around to see what she could find that she might use to free herself.

Someone must have seen her following Omar Selim back to the house and then had waited around to see if she came back. When she had, they had conked her on the noggin and trussed her up like a Christmas goose! Omar was in cahoots with somebody and she intended to find out who! Her questing fingers found her pocketbook and Grace smiled around the gag as she pulled it open and began to search inside. A fingernail file! She got it out and began sawing at the ropes that bound her wrists.

"So you have this mess figured out?" Corky asked as he, Jimmy and Nick left the Hanging Monkey in search of Grace. The Monkey chattered at them as they passed it. Nick looked up, paused for a moment and then nodded.

"I do, but I want everyone together when I explain it," Nick said. "Did Grace happen to say anything that might tell you where she had been?"

"Well, I had a bit of a run-in with Doohan today and the Monkey had raised quite a ruckus when he arrived and then again when he left. Yon beastie never has liked him and the feeling seems to be mutual on Doohan's side," Corky replied.

"Has it ever reacted that way with anyone else?" Nick looked thoughtful.

"That's what the wee lassie asked and I told her he reacted that way only at Omar Selim. That greasy little crook even gives me the creeps," Corky shrugged.

"Where does Omar Selim live?" Nick asked urgently.

"A small cottage at the edge of town," Corky shrugged.

"You don't think Grace would have…" Jimmy let it trail off as the three men looked at each other and then they all broke into a run. Nick was convinced if Grace had gone to Omar's place that she was in danger!

Nick thumbed on a flashlight as they approached the house, and the white beam lanced through the darkness, catching a dark-clad figure preparing to enter the building. At their approach the figure darted into the shadows.

"I've got him," Jimmy said, drawing his revolver and heading after the man.

"The door is open," Corky pointed out, as they moved closer.

"It is," Nick nodded, drawing his Colt .45 automatic. He held the flash in one hand and the gun in the other. Corky had drawn his own pistol as well. Carefully the two men entered the house. "Grace!" Nick called softly as they moved inside. There was a noise from a back room.

"I heard, lad," Corky whispered. The Irishman reached for the doorknob and twisted it and threw the door open. The flashlight cut through the darkness and bathed a very rumpled and angry-looking Grace Thomas sitting in its light. Corky swung into the room, feeling along the wall for the light switch, flipping it on. A bare bulb flared to light.

"Grace," Nick said, dropping to his knees and opening his pocket knife. The keenly edged blade sliced through the rope in seconds and he helped remove the gag from her mouth.

"What the devil took you so long?" Grace asked after he pulled the gag from her mouth.

"It's not like you left directions," Nick shook his head, grinning, glad that he had found her in time.

"I hate to interrupt, but we have other problems," Corky didn't sound especially happy.

"What now?" Nick asked.

"Another dead body," Corky pointed with his gun. Omar Selim was crumpled in a corner, his throat cut and a pool of blood surrounding his body.

"Oh, my!" Grace nearly shrieked.

"What is it with you and dead bodies? Everywhere you go they start turning up," Nick took out a cigarette and fired it up. He blew out a cloud of blue smoke.

"Let me have one, please," Grace commanded her voice trembling. Nick handed her his and she drew on it deeply before, exhaling the smoke. Nick fired up another Lucky Strike for himself.

Jimmy Dolan came bursting into the house. "He got away in the jungle. Is Grace okay?" Jimmy asked.

"She is; Omar's a little worse for wear," Nick said disgustedly.

"Oh, crap!" Jimmy exploded.

"Nick, I've been thinking. We need to find Doohan," Grace said.

"You want to make a withdrawal from the bank?" Jimmy gave her an odd look.

"What she means is that Doohan is our killer," Nick told him.

"What?" Corky and Dolan gasped at once.

"The monkey was raising a ruckus when Burke was killed. It only does that when Doohan or Selim was around. I think Doohan and Selim were in on it together and Doohan got greedy. He wanted to keep the jewel for himself," Nick explained.

"What jewel?" Grace asked.

"The Eye of Ka. It was stolen from an idol on Papogo Island by Burke," Nick explained.

"We need to get this information to Colonel Smythe," Corky said.

"He knows most of it, except for the fact that Doohan is the killer," Nick replied.

"But who has the jewel?" Grace asked.

"I think I know the answer to that, as well," Nick said, helping her up.

"So are you going to share?" Grace asked him.

"When we get back to the Monkey," Nick replied.

"What about Doohan?" Jimmy asked.

"He'll turn up. It's not that big of an island," Nick sighed.

Together the four of them walked back to the Hanging Monkey. The noise was less festive than it had been before they left and the air was filled with a sense of dangerous anticipation. The Papogo, tribesmen stood on one side of the bar, looking over the other patrons in a way that made them very uncomfortable. Colonel Smythe was wiping his brow with an already damp handkerchief.

Khuna was standing watch and keeping both sides at bay. Chi Pei was also in the bar. The tall Chinese was very imposing given his great height and glittering green eyes. The flowing green robe that swirled around him seemed almost alive.

"Glad to see you found her," Colonel Smythe announced as they entered the bar.

"We found another dead body, as well. Omar Selim is dead," Nick replied, keeping an eye on Chi Pei in an effort to gauge his reaction. It seemed to catch the Oriental by surprise.

"Bloody hell!" Smythe exploded.

"We also know who's behind it all, too," Nick cut in.

"Do tell, Mister Fortune," Chi Pei's voice was as sibilant as a snake.

"Who?" Smythe demanded. The bar had fallen totally silent, so much so that one could have heard a pin drop.

"Poke Doohan," Nick said, naming the banker. There was a commotion outside and the Scottish banker burst through the doors, a pistol in his hand.

"You're a liar, Nick Fortune!" Doohan roared. He raised his gun but Nick Fortune was faster, firing his Colt from the hip. The heavy slug caught the banker in the chest and hurled him back through the batwing doors.

"But what of the jewel? Does Doohan possess the Eye of Ka?" Chi Pei asked. Some of the Papogo Islanders moved towards him, knives filling their hands.

"No. The jewel was taken before Doohan had a chance at it," Nick replied.

"By whom?" Khuna asked, eyeing the cannibals warily.

"By Doohan's nemesis, the monkey," Nick replied. He walked outside, followed by the others. The monkey dropped lightly onto his shoulders and handed him something, then leaped back into the trees. Nick turned and offered the stone to Khuna. The Motugran Warrior took the stone and presented it to the Chief of the Papogo tribe. The cannibals filed past the rest and headed for their boats.

"Can't say I'm not glad to see them go," Jake Sloan took a drink of beer.

"Me. either," Colonel Smythe added.

"Very interesting presentation, Mr. Fortune. I shall have to keep an eye on you," Chi Pei said, and then he vanished down the boardwalk towards the docks as well.

"Well, Gracie, you certainly have a story now," Corky O'Brian said.

"That I do," Grace agreed.

"Let's all go get a drink," Nick said, and they turned and went back inside. Smythe had a couple of his men remove Doohan's body. The monkey sat on the branch, grinning as the night wore on.

The End

Tales from the Hanging Monkey

I was a big fan of a TV show starring Stephen Collins in the 1980s called *Tales of the Gold Monkey*. It was TV's answer to Indiana Jones who was finding big success at the box office in that decade. It followed the exploits of a former "Flying Tiger," who was now flying cargo around in the Marivella Islands before WW2. It had just been released on DVD back last spring and they were having an island theme going on at work. One of the Operations Managers sent a message out to everyone's computers that told a specific person how to reach his desk. It read, "My desk is at the end of the row just behind the Hanging Monkey." It stuck in my head and I pitched the idea to Ron Fortier at Airship 27. I said what if...and then before long I had all of these wonderful characters running around in my head with stories screaming to be told. Amazingly enough, Ron said yes and then I went to work on "The Eye of Ka," which established firm roles for all of the main characters. It was a combination mystery story and adventure. I am already more than halfway through my story for the second book of Monkey Tales, which is again a creepy mystery/adventure tale that adds even more depth to the characters and their relationships. I do this between working on the further adventures of Hardluck Hannigan and the Decker P.I. mysteries. I enjoy writing these South Sea Island adventures because they are pure pulp fun and they give me a chance to play in a brand new sandbox....

BILL CRAIG is a long-time pulp aficionado who grew up on Doc Savage and The Shadow as well as The Spider. He loves the writing style of these old pulps and the tales of high adventure and decided that was what he wanted to write at the age of six. He published his first novel, *Valley of Death: A Jack Riley Adventure,* in 2000. Craig often states it only took him thirty four years to become an overnight success as a writer. Now, with twenty novels under his belt, as well as publications in two weird western anthologies is branching out. His goal is to break Walter B. Gibson's world record for the most words written in a single year.... Bill is also the single dad of three grown children and one very energetic six year old of whom he has sole custody. He also has seven grand children and takes care of his eighty-four year old father. His plate is full, but writing helps him get through each day!

MOTUGRA'S REVENGE

By Tommy Hancock

Rotten fruit. That's what Khuna was reminded of. An overripe mango blackened with bruise and decay kicked and batted about with a stick by native children. The fruit, belching and popping, its thin, leathery skin splitting, fetid flesh and juice vomiting from within. Khuna tensed his thick, taut arms once more, muscles bulging under his ebony skin, rearing up like snakes ready to strike. Khuna exhaled, matching the dying breath of the man across from him. He leaned forward, up on the balls of his bare feet, and shoved the spear his father had taught him to fight with one more thrust. That was when he was reminded of children playing with rotten mango fruit. When he felt the spearhead give as it pierced his foe's heart, slicing the organ in two as if it were a sausage.

As the corpse—clothed from head to toe, except for a slit in the cloth mask he wore showing now dead eyes—collapsed, Khuna grunted, shook the spear, and with a deft kick dispatched his kill from its shaft. He turned swiftly, spinning the spear above his head, bringing it around to grasp it with both hands as a defensive weapon. The body of his attacker fell to the thatch and mud floor of Khuna's hut with a lifeless smack, but the islander's ears ignored it. Eyes closed, Khuna listened for other things. Sounds outside of the shack he'd built near the Hanging Monkey, a place much like the one belonging to his family in his village, an escape from the incessant cricket-like roar of the crowd in the bar, and from Corky's ribald stories and off key Irish ballads. His ears reached outside of the bamboo walls, listening, as his diminutive, yet muscular body rolled into a crouch, his left leg jutted out to the left his weight on his bent right leg, waiting. All because of what Khuna knew. A singular truth common to all creatures, be it tiger or man.

Cowards who attack in the dark of night never ever come alone.

Stepping over the dead man without looking at him and with the grace of a ghost, Khuna receded into the shadows of his own domicile.

His onyx eyes narrowed, aimed at the planks and bamboo poles he and Jimmy Dolan had lashed together to make a door. Minutes passed and Khuna listened, at first to nothing but the inherent sounds of the night, an orphan bird squawk to the west, the tickling hum of a breeze stumbling in off the Pacific. Then other noises rose, brush rustling, dirt and sand being kicked up by men, hints of labored breathing. There were two of them, Khuna determined. Men convinced they were as silent as attacking cobras, but actually to the ears of a Motugran, making more noise than drunk toucans falling out of breadfruit trees.

He'd known they would come when their friend, the leader of the pack of human dogs most likely, did not return. Khuna grimaced, disgusted with men such as these, those who claimed to be warriors but were little more than scavengers gathering at the feet of whoever paid or cajoled them into service, rats waiting to feed on the dead carcasses they intended to leave in their wakes. The one lying prostrate just a few feet from Khuna, his blood filling the small hut with the metallic tinge of death, had something to prove, either to those he pretended to lead or to his own master or even to himself. Khuna did not care. All the fool had proven was he could die like any other man.

The roughly crafted door swung open and started to shut again, but the figure outlined by moonlight behind him stopped it. He was a tall man, thin like a fence rail, with both arms raised. His left hand hovered near his black masked face, clenched in a fist while his right hand led him in, black-gloved fingers wrapped around the hilt of a finely polished hunting knife.

"'e in there, George?" The voice came from behind the gangly man, a raspy whinny, high pitched, yet edged with gravel. Khuna had heard men like this many times, their voices ravaged by years of life on boat decks inhaling the salty air of the sea. "What do ye see?"

"Body." George replied with a guttural whisper. "Just one."

"'ell!" swore George's still unseen companion. "Maybe 'e's not even been here yet and someone else killed the dirty islander."

"No," George said, stepping cautiously out of the doorway, allowing Khuna to see his partner finally. Wearing a black full-body uniform of some sort just like George and the other man, this one resembled a fleshy beer keg with tree stumps for legs. He, too held a knife as crisp and cleanly shined as George's in one hand but his other hand, though it trembled like a shivering ham, held something squat, black, and ugly. A pistol.

"Jiminy damn," George swore, stopping about halfway across the floor of the shack. Khuna pressed himself back against the far wall, sinking even further into the cloak of darkness hanging from it. "It's Peters all right." George stood, stretching his full six feet tall and looked up, searching for something. "I think he goofed, Miley. I think Peters woke up the wrong native and got his chest skewered for it."

"Wrong one?" Miley squealed. Then he turned his bulging yellow eyes to follow George's gaze. "Oh," he said, "I get it. I don't see it neither, George."

"Do you," Khuna snarled, his right arm grabbing at something on the ground beside him and snapping outward like a whip, slinging what he held at the two men, "look for this?"

The fat one named Miley yelped like a wounded hound as he staggered backwards, fear driving him into retreat. His feet slammed into one another, bringing him down to the ground in a trembling heap. George sidestepped what was thrown at him and let it slap the ground with a fleshy splat. He put one foot behind him, lowered his shoulders, and raised his blade. He didn't have to look at what lay near him to know what it was. He'd hung the thing in the middle of Khuna's shack earlier in the evening while the native was in O'Brian's bar.

It was a dead monkey. Hair the color of midnight, its coat dull, all luster—like its very life—gone. The creature's tail jutted out behind it stiffly. A hole gaped in the tail about two inches from its tip, where George had driven the nail earlier to hang it for Khuna to find.

"Listen, island boy," George derided. "No need to act like we're a warrin' tribe or something, like you did with Peters here." George paused, waiting for a reply. All he heard was Miley's ragged breathing behind him. "We just come to bring you a message."

From the seemingly endless black in the corner of the hut flew something else. A slender blade, its hilt nothing more than blackened leather wrapped around the steel, sunk deep into the monkey corpse. "Your message," Khuna retorted, his voice deep and resonant, as if the night itself were speaking, "has been received."

"Move, George," Miley whispered as if Khuna could not hear him. "I'll get 'im," the fat intruder promised, using both meaty hands to hold his gun. The barrel danced around as it quivered in time with Miley's terrified body, rolls of fat shivering under black cloth.

George opened his mouth to say something, but words vanished as the shadows in the hut seemed to coalesce in the corner before him. Two hands grasping a long spear fired at George, some part of the spear shaft striking his face, knocking him to the ground. Khuna leaped over George as he fell and let the spear slide through his hands. Miley screamed like a violated child and fired blindly, his bullet striking Peters' already clearly expired cadaver. As the bullet left the barrel, Khuna slapped the gun with the head of his spear, knocking it out of Miley's grasp and across the shack.

Landing against the door, Khuna whirled about, spear raised, body poised to attack again. Miley blubbered, trying to crawl his way to safety, but stopped short as he came upon the two dead bodies. He cried, tears and sweat mingling on his face, and he halted in horror on all fours, stricken still with terror.

Taking no notice of his partner, George pulled his thin form up off the ground and, hunting knife drawn up over his head to strike, lunged for Khuna. Growling like an offended cat, George swiped the blade at his enemy, slicing only air. He drew back to strike again and advance, but Khuna's answer to his first attack ended the battle. With a speed George would never see again, Khuna sprang at him, his spear in one hand, the other suddenly wrapped around George's wrist, the one that held the hunting knife. Like an ebon lightning bolt, Khuna yanked fiercely on George's wrist, bringing the knife down savagely, burying it hilt deep in George's chest.

In shock and agony, George relaxed his grip on the knife. As he staggered, Khuna took hold of the knife's hilt and, in one fluid motion, jerked the knife upward, ending whatever life George had left, and then withdrew the blade, crimson with blood. Shoving past the dead man as he fell to the ground, Khuna tangled his strong fingers in the cloth mask the paralyzed Miley wore. A shrill screech left the traumatized man's lips as Khuna tore the mask from his head, revealing pale white skin, heavy jowls, three chins, and a mop of sweat-soaked yellow hair. Taking Miley's sodden yellow locks in his iron grip, Khuna stood astride him and from behind raised the fat man's head, sliding the purloined knife against his obscenely fleshy neck. Miley wet himself as he heard George's blood drip from the blade that would soon likely wear his as well.

"Muh…muh…puh…puh…." Miley had no words, not even to beg for the rotten remnant of existence he called a life.

"Speak," Khuna insisted, his voice a throaty, torturous itch against Miley's right ear, "and live. But speak only what I wish to hear."

A tremor went through Miley's weighty frame, every inch of his body coated in fear-induced perspiration. He mumbled again, trying to form words to lie and plead, but all dishonesty fled from his mind as he felt the wet coldness of the bloody knife on his neck.

"Only…did it…" he stammered, unsure if he knew how to talk any longer, "I only went along with it...for a place to eat...and sleep. I'm... I'm not like Peters and George...not like the others...I just...was between boats...a long time...."

Not satisfied, Khuna pressed the knife a bit harder against Miley's neck. "What message do you bring?"

"That...that you were to come...." Miley gasped for breath, fright overriding his most basic functions. He choked, trying to force air in and out of lungs that wanted to be anywhere but in his chest. "He...left the monkeys...to remind...you...and the others....Remind...of what you did to him...."

"Come?" Khuna parroted, noting the rest of Miley's desperate words. "Come where?"

"To...to him....He has...three...of you...of the others...He wants the rest...to come...."

Khuna growled in Miley's ear, making the man quake even more. Too many questions and suddenly, Khuna realized, very little time to ask them. As he decided what step to take next, he glanced and noticed something on Miley's arm, on the shoulder of his left sleeve; a dash of red with black emblazoned on top of it. Recognition fired in his mind, lighting up at least part of the mystery. Taking the knife away from Miley's neck, but not relaxing his hold on his hair, Khuna asked, "Who is he?"

Miley blubbered, tears outnumbering drops of sweat, his eyes red with crying. He felt the blade dig into his arm, nicking his skin. Knowing this savage was about to eviscerate him, to butcher him like a calf, the fat sailor screamed, "Motugra!"

Nick Fortune hated being nervous. A man who had stared down Nazi submarines, shotgun wielding fathers, and islanders eager to boil his head down to size absolutely despised the uneasiness anxiety brought on him. It wasn't often that he got that little teasing tickle on the back of his neck that sent every hair to attention; he just simply wouldn't allow it. Anxiety for Nick meant fear, even though the woman, windstorm, or wrongdoing hadn't been crafted yet that could give Fortune a case of the frights. Still, there were times in his life, moments when the iron will he exerted over himself did him about as much good as the left eye he no longer had. Five of them, Fortune mused as he walked down the wooden boardwalk leading from the collection of buildings and lost souls some on Motugra called a town. Five instances where Fortune's nerves all fired off warnings at once, giving him eerie feelings, paranoia by the pound, and a sense of dread no undertaker could match.

"Hellfire," Fortune cursed, his fingers teasing the butt of his holstered Browning 9mm as he stealthily approached the bar he nearly called home. "Make that six."

He'd left the Hanging Monkey little more than two hours before. Although a regular, this particular night he'd not planned to grace the watering hole, even though both Corky O'Brian and Jimmy Dolan excitedly encouraged him to come earlier in the day. It seemed that Corky woke up to a startling surprise that morning in his apartment at the back of the Monkey. That shock being the nomenclature of his bar made real. Suspended just over O'Brian's head, tied to a dirty blade of his wicker fan with a leather strap while he snored a few bars of Bolero, was a monkey. A dead monkey. To hear O'Brian tell it, this strange occurrence didn't faze him at all. Jimmy Dolan's version, however, was that he, while helping Miko with one of her projects in the bar proper, heard O'Brian caterwaul like he'd become a banshee his own self and explode out of his apartment in nothing but a pair of skivvies, waving a black haired spider monkey cadaver to and fro like a lantern signaling a train. Corky was so verklempt over the whole affair, according to Dolan, that he'd almost missed the note that was tied about the poor little beast's neck. Some gibberish, O'Brian had said, about 'the night the Hanging Monkey defeated' some such or other.

The Hanging Monkey now sat before Fortune in the early morning darkness like a clapboard and bamboo lion resting on its haunches, its shingled mane relaxed. It was a sight that Nick Fortune had seen in various states of consciousness and more than once had thought he'd never see again. Viewing Corky O'Brian's interesting establishment did not itself inspire Fortune's nervousness. It was the fact that no lights at all shone from the Monkey. Not one. It didn't matter that it was very nearly four o'clock in the morning. Fortune had never known Corky to leave the Monkey totally dark, usually because the big Irish mook would forget and leave a light burning or Miko and Khuna, unable to get the last remaining lush to wash away on his own, locked said lush in and left a light for him to snore by.

Fortune had no intention, even after hearing about the yank someone had given Corky's tail, of darkening the Monkey's door that day. Not until

Dolan stepped on his boat just after noon. Both Miko and Jimmy thought it strange, what had happened to Corky, and spent over an hour denying any part in it. Still, they both chalked it up to some rummy on the island that Corky had angered, which Corky was well known to do. That is, until Dolan went to the hangar where his beloved lady of the sky spent her time when not flying above the island and found a monkey all his own, note and all, hanging from the propeller of his Grumman Goose. Not by its tail, Dolan explained, because orangutans don't have tails. Fortune had thought it funny that Dolan saw fit to explain that to him in his recitation, but didn't address the fact that orangutans didn't normally haunt the jungles of Motugra. Instead this deceased primate dangled by its own hands, locked somehow in a death grip on one of the propeller's blades.

As he moved slowly up the boardwalk toward the bar, Fortune noticed more plainly the second thing that currently caused him grief. The front door of the Hanging Monkey was one thick bulwark. Not much to look at, the portal proved effective nonetheless, essentially a massive block of wood cut to fit its respective doorframe. The door was so heavy that no one except Khuna in his role as O'Brian's keeper of the peace could hold it open very long. The bar sat on just enough of a slope that the door would not remain open on its own. Not unless something was in the way keeping it from closing, something large enough to be unmovable.

Like the body Fortune spied in the doorway. A man with his arms thrown wide, his head lolled away from Nick's view.

This made, Nick counted in his head as he decided what to do next, the fifth dead thing he'd seen today. Nolan coaxed him off his boat and, at this moment, Fortune wished he'd never left Fortune's Folly to go to a viewing for dead monkeys. But he had and found himself the first time that day in the Hanging Monkey in mid-afternoon, standing around a table in the center of the establishment. Corky, Miko, Khuna, and Dolan all stood vigil with him over what lay on top of the table—three deceased monkeys. Corky's spider monkey lay beside Dolan's orangutan, which occupied most of the tabletop. On the other side of the larger animal, appearing as if it was nuzzling against the orangutan, lay a much smaller monkey. Putting Fortune in mind of the squirrels that haunted his grandmother's oak trees when he was a child, this monkey had gray fur, tufts of white sprouting at its ears and a dollop of white on the forehead of its hairless face. It was a marmoset, Miko had said, and it was the one that had been left for her, swinging back and forth in front of the door to her room. Yet another note had accompanied this slender tree climber.

Sliding his gun from its home, Fortune tugged his captain's hat down hard, a single curl of brown hair still visible under its brim, and walked on. As he neared the door, he drifted to the right, up against the Hanging Monkey's wall. Looking down, he didn't recognize the obviously dead man holding the door open. Shreds of black cloth, what was left of some sort of mask, clung to his bloody face, cuts and wounds marking him from the crown of his head to his chin. Nick turned his attention to the hands, both gloved, but the left one with a kitchen knife through its palm. It was the knife Miko normally used to cut lemons and onions.

Fortune felt it, that accursed tingle that something was not only not right, but had gone horribly wrong. The same sensation sent him bolting out of the Hanging Monkey earlier after hearing about Miko's monkey headed straight for Grace Thomas' room in the Wickersham Hotel. He arrived at her door just as Grace did, having been interviewing the fourth island governor Motugra had had in six months. Without explaining, Fortune took her key and opened the door. He saw nothing amiss; no dead monkey. Then Grace, laughing at Fortune's tomfoolery, went to the closet and pulled back the linen curtain in front of it. Fortune couldn't suppress a grin when the tough as nails lady correspondent shrilled like a little girl at the sight of the once stunning golden lion tamarin, its brilliant orange hair now dull, its once prominent mane limp, nearly hiding its black face. As he worked the body off of the hanger to which it had been tied, Fortune showed no surprise when his fingers brushed a note tied around its neck, masked by the drooping mane.

Unsure of what awaited him inside the cavernous bar, Fortune chose to make as little commotion as possible. Stepping over the body, he turned and worked his way in. He slammed his left elbow into the monolith of a door and bit hard into his lower lip, curtailing the litany of swears that instantly rose at the onset of pain. Unsure if the thunk of his arm colliding with the door would bring curious eyes or, worse yet, hot lead, Fortune raised his gun, ready from an attack from all sides.

Except above.

Fortune's ears caught the hum of something swinging in the air too late as two feet struck him dead center in the chest. As every breath he'd planned to take for the next five minutes erupted from his mouth, Fortune flew backward, glancing off the partially open door. Having been surprised before, Fortune, even in the heat of the moment, willed himself to hold onto the only thing that might save his life. His thin, but firm fingers instinctively clinched the butt of his Browning, as if they embraced a lover about to leave them. Still functioning on reflex alone, Fortune pushed against the door, jumping back on his feet, bringing his gun around all at the same time. Even the death grip Fortune wished he'd had on his weapon could not withstand the double kicks of his assailant. He saw the shadowy figure turn a flip in front of him and deftly kick the gun out of his hand with one foot, the other slapping him as if it were a fist on the chin. Again, Fortune fell, this time against nothing but the hard slab of the bar floor. He heard the clatter of his gun skittering across the floor and, determined to retrieve it and even the playing field, started to climb back up to his feet, only to find his attacker looming over him. His single eye, adjusted finally to the inky blackness within the Monkey, could make out a figure. A nicely defined, curvaceous one. A decidedly familiar figure.

"Miko!"

"Nick?" The declaration of his name came an instant before a proffered hand, one he knew to be the yellow of autumn leaves and delicate, yet home to five of the deadliest fingers he'd ever held. As he grasped the hand, pushing himself to his feet with his other arm planted on the floor, Miko continued, "You shouldn't really sneak up on a girl like that in the dark, Fortune."

"Most of the women," Fortune spat sarcastically, blood trickling out of his lips with his words, "I sneak up on don't come from—" He stopped, realizing he had a question. "Just where exactly did you come from, Miko?"

Miko, a slight wisp of a woman, gestured with a slim arm. "Beam runs across the bar right above the door. After the last one fell, I needed a place to wait to see if any more came." The smile on her face was evident in her words, though Fortune couldn't see it. "I didn't know I was going to get the opportunity most women who come in here end up wanting after a few hours with you, Nick."

Under normal circumstances, Fortune would have jibed back at Miko, both of them honing their sarcastic wits on one another. But nothing was normal about a day of dead monkeys and missing people. "The last one? How many other than the door stop?"

In answer to his query, the approximately ten bulbs that normally provided the scant lighting in the Hanging Monkey crackled and sparked to life. Miko now stood behind the bar where the switch to the generator was camouflaged. She wore what Nick assumed was something she threw on in a hurry, a pair of canvas pants and a white shirt, tails out, a man's shirt. Fortune shook his head, amazed at how soundlessly and effortlessly the tavern's resident Jill-of-all-trades moved. The boat captain registered a bit more surprise, realizing that Miko had had to navigate two overturned tables, four splintered chairs, and three unconscious or dead men all lying prone in their own unique positions between where he stood and the bar where she now leaned, a Cheshire grin across her finely featured face.

"I know," Fortune started, working his own way through the maze of broken furniture and men to the long mahogany tinted bar, "that Corky usually leaves you to do the tidying up, Miko, but I can't believe he'd miss out on a chance to...."

"Corky's gone." Miko's voice was even, almost calm, but Fortune saw the torrent of rage burning in her almond eyes. "I had left for the night, to my room in town. I came back here. I guess there'd been three or four more. They'd left with Corky already, according to the first one you met at the door." Something shifted in her voice, something that gave Fortune a chill. "He, and these others, they've gone to their God now," Miko said harshly, "His last words were about them taking Corky. And begging for just one more day."

Knowing there was no use or time to walk that trail, Fortune instead set off another way. "They took Corky? It must have been an army of goons with arms like cast iron anchors to waylay that Irishman."

"You forget," Miko said. "It's Wednesday. The third Wednesday of the month."

Fortune had forgotten. He'd seen Corky earlier in the evening, nearly three hours ago, and still it hadn't registered. Because that was just part of the package, what made the owner of the Hanging Monkey who he was. As long as Corky had been on the island, he'd never been known to get so drunk that he couldn't pour a headless draught or fight four men to a standstill. Except, for a reason known only to the burly brawling Irishman, the third Wednesday of each month. Everyone on Motugra had secrets and everyone had their own way of dealing with them. Corky O'Brian's solution was drinking himself into stark oblivion the third Wednesday of every month.

"Hellfire," Fortune fumed between gritted teeth. "They probably just carted the big lug out of his bed. Still probably took four or five to carry all that Irish out of here." Before Miko could respond, Fortune kept on, his voice now heavy with fury and hints of vengeance. "Grace is gone."

Miko's face flushed with anguish, quickly replaced by stoic anger. "Nick...."

"Miko…now leaned, a Chesire grin across her…face."

"When Jimmy and I left, you know, a while ago, we went to check on Grace. Everyone was still here then. Hell, Corky was still tilting mugs and slinging shots. I don't know about you, but I'd pretty much decided that the dead monkey thing was—I don't know what. Anyway, in case there was something going on, Jimmy and I decided to make sure Grace was at the Wickersham. I'd tried to get her to stay here, but she had to be bull stubborn and leave an hour earlier.

"We made our way to the hotel, Jimmy picking on me the whole walk, asking how it felt to be the only one of our merry band who didn't get gifted an expired zoo exhibit. I ignored it mostly, but by the time we reached the Wickersham, something nagged at me, made me have to make sure Grace was okay."

"But she wasn't," Miko assumed as if she somehow knew the rest of the story.

Fortune shook his head. "Her door was busted up, broken down. She put up one helluva tussle it looked like, chairs topsy-turvy, mirror broken. But her window, it was open. Somehow whoever snatched her took her out of that room, over the balcony and down three floors on a single hemp rope knotted around the balcony railing."

"Grace would not have gone were she able to fight back," Miko said somberly.

"Yeah," Fortune grimly agreed. "I know."

"Neither," Miko uttered, "would have Jimmy."

Fortune cocked his head, raising an eyebrow, enough of a response to urge Miko on. "I came back here, Nick, because I knew something was wrong. Jimmy was supposed to meet me," She hesitated, then forged on. "He was supposed to meet me in my room." Her brown eyes searched Fortune's face for some sort of reaction, but found nothing. Maybe she and Dolan had not kept their secret as well as she'd thought. "I didn't know about Grace, but that must have been what made him late. I dressed to go in search of him, but as I did, my eyes caught a flash of something outside my window. It was Jimmy, two men in black holding him by his arms, and another..." her words faltered, but when she spoke again, they dripped with fervor, "another hitting him. Over and over in the stomach."

"I was out of the house and in the back in less than a minute, Nick, but they were gone. Nothing was there. Not Jimmy. Not those three. Nothing. Except blood."

Nick Fortune slammed a clenched fist hard against the bar top. The crack of knuckles against the wood reverberated off the bar's walls, but it was not foolish pain that marred the movie star features of the sailor. It was confusion and anger. Nothing made sense—not the monkeys, not the notes, not the men in black—but something was going on. Corky, Jimmy, Grace. Only Miko was left. Miko and ...

"Khuna!" Fortune shouted as he turned wildly, his eyes searching the floor for his Browning. Dashing across the room to retrieve it, he said, "He's the only one of our merry band of rogues and drunkards that we don't know about." Bending over, he scooped his pistol off the concrete. "When did he leave here?"

"No matter, Fortune. I have returned."

Both Miko and Nick startled at the resonant thunder of the native's voice echoing from behind them. With all of her skills, even Miko stood in hidden awe of Khuna, how he moved with the silence of the island wind, how the very earth itself seemed to work to mask his every step, to leave no trace he was ever anywhere behind. He melted from the shadows at the back of the Hanging Monkey, his pitch skin taking on nuances of light as he moved into view.

"Khuna," Miko asked, "Did you find...."

"Yes." Khuna raised his arm, his hand holding the now stiff howler monkey corpse from his room by its damaged tail. Gently placing the animal on the bar, Khuna said, "I waited, for I knew those who had left this were not far. They would return. They did, first one wanting to take me, to make me go." Khuna's hard onyx eyes flickered with an obscene ebony spark all their own. "I said no, he tried to force me. He died. So did one of the others."

Miko nodded. "That is what happened here as well. Except," Miko looked over the bar, a sort of childlike gleam in her eyes, "all of mine died."

"Hellfire," Fortune barked as he marched to the bar, circled the end of it, and made himself at home by snatching a bottle of rotgut, one of O'Brian's specialty brands, from the floor under the bar. As he uncapped the whiskey, he said, "All right. So this has to do with the five of you and somehow I got off scot-free. Except for the fact of givin' a gull's feathers about you lot. Guilty by association, I guess." Fortune ignored the shot glass Miko had reached across the bar and now held out to him. Taking his dose from the neck of the bottle, he cleared the fire from his throat. "I think we'll also agree there'll be no going to the local gendarme for this one."

Miko chuckled. "Gilhooley? That kid is no more policeman than I am

Vivien Leigh. He just rambled out of here a few hours ago, ranting about joining his country's army and seeing the world. Be surprised if he's on the island much longer."

"This," Khuna decreed, "is our war." He cut his piercing gaze at Fortune, "No one else's."

"Sorry, big guy," Fortune quipped, "but I've already misplaced an intrepid girl reporter and took three or four kicks to my solar plexus and above. I've paid my fare for this ride."

"Too many questions," Miko remarked, ignoring the verbal sparring of the only two living men in the room. "And so much effort to make mystery. Monkeys. Notes. Men in black coming...."

"The notes!" Fortune exclaimed, his cheeks flushing slightly for not thinking of it earlier. "Khuna, your monkey had one?"

Khuna extended his left hand, one that Fortune was sure had been open before, but now closed in a fist. As the lithe, lethal fingers blossomed apart, nestled in the native's palm was a rolled piece of white parchment.

"Good," Fortune cheered, jamming one hand into his pants pocket, fishing around for a moment, then pulling out a crumpled scrap. "This is Grace's. She gave it to me, making a big joke out of it. 'In case something happens to me, Nick,' she said." His voice trailed off.

"Jimmy's I have," Miko added, offering no explanation why she would have Dolan's cryptic communication. "Mine, too. And Corky's..." she rounded the bar, crossed behind Fortune and bent over, her dainty hands fumbling through the half-full oil drum that Corky used for a garbage can. "Here," she said, "right on top where the mighty O'Brian flung it before falling into his third Wednesday stupor." Before she was fully upright, Miko's fingers had yanked and pulled the wad of paper back into its full, albeit wrinkled, length.

"Up here," Fortune ordered, placing Grace's note on the bar top. When the other four joined their mate, the three companions studied them, each one trying to force the pieces of the puzzle into a whole picture, an image that might unlock the madness behind the last twenty-four hours.

"They make no sense," Miko surmised after studying each one as they were displayed on the bar. "Ravings of a lunatic."

"Yeah," Fortune confirmed. "Except they're all signed the same way: 'Motugra.' Didn't know the island had it in for all of you."

"There was order," Khuna said, "to all of this. And there is order to these."

"Order," Miko repeated. Her face brightened with realization and, without saying anything, her hands swiftly pushed the notes around, like paper boats on a wooden ocean. Sliding one to the left, moving another between two more. "There," Miko chirped after a minute or so of shuffling. "Like Khuna said, there is an order."

The notes were now lined up vertically, Corky's recently trashed missive being the first, followed by Dolan's, Miko's, Grace's, and finally Khuna's. All in the order they were delivered, attached somehow to their grotesque messengers, five dead hanging monkeys.

From top to bottom the five notes, all signed 'Motugra' read:

"You and Yours attended me the Night the Hanging Monkey defeated my Dreams...

"Youth and Drink made You blind to the Good I Would do For All ...

"Your lotus blossom of a hand ended My Life with One Strike...

"Words were Arrows You Slung and broke My Very Spirit...

"Dark Hands Soiled Me. Me who would be this Island. Me who Could Be this world."

Fortune whistled as he pushed his captain's cap back on his head, letting loose a few unruly strands of brown. "One thing stands out. Whoever our friend is, he's several wheels shy of a wagon."

"Still," Miko countered, her exquisite face twisted in confusion and recollection, "this, all of this touches some memory for me. Something that happened...here. And how they're signed. 'Motugra.' That's familiar as well."

"This then," Khuna interjected, his left hand again held out, palm open this time, a scrap of cloth lying where the paper had before, "will cause the sun itself to rise."

Fortune took hold of the tattered piece with two fingers, almost dropping it when he realized it was heavy and wet. "Blood?" Fortune asked as he laid the remnant beside the notes.

"Only," Khuna replied, a hint of humor in his voice, "because he who wore it would not sit still. I cut it from his arm and then he fled. Back to the sea. Back to the ships."

"Probably half way to Hawaii now," Fortune jabbed, "under his own steam."

"No," Khuna added, a smile widening on his face. "Too much of the pig in that one."

Miko flattened the cloth out for all to see. Ragged around the edges, it was a circle of red cloth with images in black thread sewn into it. Two lines appeared first to form a tiny X in the center of the red field, but if one looked closer, the swastika the lines formed became clearer. Most of the patch, though, was dominated by a stylized letter, thick black thread in a stylistic old script, rising from the lower left of the patch, up to the top, back down, up again, and ending at the lower right. An easily recognizable, large capital 'M.'

"I've seen that," Fortune said, a hard edge growing in his voice. "Tonight. Walked right past it."

"Yes," Khuna agreed. "A growing blot on the body and spirit of this island."

Miko added no words, but instead moved from behind the bar and to the closest body on the floor. Kneeling down, she looked to Khuna, questions in her eyes. The islander slapped his left arm with his right hand, almost completely atop his shoulder. Miko turned back to the corpse and ran her hand up the man's left arm. As she reached the shoulder, she pushed aside a black epaulet that, running from the neck of the shirt, hung nearly two inches down the arm. There, covered by the epaulet, was a bloodless twin to the torn emblem on the bar.

"I remember," Miko said, her voice far away in recollection as she stood, "the last night he was here."

"Who?" Fortune quizzed. "Marik? The island's resident goosestepper?"

"Yes," Miko answered. "Almost a year now."

"I don't follow," Fortune badgered. "Sure, he showed up three or four years ago, crying that his boss in the Daddyland wanted him to claim Motugra as an outpost, but that went nowhere fast. He's been holed up in that old warehouse in the middle of town for months. What's he call it again?"

"The Reichstag." Miko supplied.

"Yeah," Fortune confirmed. "No one's seen much of him or anyone go in and out. Nothin' even to say what it is but that fancy M hanging over the doorway. Why would Marik have it hard for any of you?"

Miko looked at Khuna. "Because," the native said somberly, "we made him look a fool."

Rain pelted the clapboard walls of the Hanging Monkey that night, just over eleven months prior. Not the polite, gentile dollops of rain that coat New York city streets or leave a glistening sheen on London's dreary buildings. These were vicious cannonballs and mortar shells of water, lobbed unmercifully by a warring torrent of wild winds and towering thunderheads. No one would be out on Motugra . And it seemed, that particular stormy evening, everyone chose to be in one place to avoid the storm: the Hanging Monkey.

Thunder clapped as if on cue at one point when the massive front door of the bar trudged open. Khuna moved from his post on the wall by the door as he always did when it opened, his eyes recording everything about the newest arrivals, his body ready for any possibility. Every muscle tensed to attention as his dark eyes viewed the procession entering the Monkey, their charcoal gray military uniform trench coats drenched to the lining.

Unlike most military officers who fancied themselves ruling despots, Major Hermann Marik always walked in front of his entourage, a riding crop in his left gloved hand slapping his left leg in time with his walk. He was a tall man, one most would say cut a dashing figure in his uniform, at least from the neck down. Unfortunately for Marik, attention was often drawn to his rather oddly configured face. His chin jutted out like an icicle hanging from the eave of a barn, jagged and pointed. Paper-thin lips sat atop this bony protrusion, forming a mouth that was little more than a slit in the mottled white flesh of his face. Pits and scars of poor hygiene in his youth spotted his visage like craters in a minefield. His nose loomed over all of that, a hawkish beak of a thing, crooked almost like a fishhook near its tip. Eyes the size of large blue cat eye marbles bulged froglike from deep recesses in his head, all of it punctuated by a sloping forehead ending in a mangled tuft of yellow hair perched on the apex of his nearly pointed skull. The hat he wore, regardless of it being his military issue or a more civilian fedora, always sat at a cockeyed angle, one Marik's men insisted was 'rakish,' but every one else saw as funny and awkward.

Four men accompanied Marik into the bar, a man who despite his freakish countenance commanded almost total loyalty from his men. These four plus ten others he'd brought with him to the island were his 'detachment,' as he'd called them when arriving in a lackluster fanfare a few years before. No one paid him any more mind when he declared he was dispatched to Motugra by the Führer himself than they had when the American representative or the Chinese Consul member showed up with similar claims of possession of the island. Since being on the island, however, Marik had managed to double his numbers of soldiers and devotees, using the words of Hitler to woo and seduce the no accounts and roustabouts that often floated to the beach on various boats to take up step with Marik. Anyone who called Motugra home knew what the major was selling was bilge water, but enough men passing through Motugra looking for glory and fortune fell victim to the siren's song of the Nazi Party.

Marik strode across the bar as if it were his own abode, like the old tin and bamboo warehouse where he'd set up shop in the middle of town when he first arrived. He'd taken to treating Motugra as a whole in much the same way during the last year or so, acting as if he were indeed governor of the swatch of land plopped out in the middle of the South Pacific. He'd been heard to say that he was now as much Motugra as he was Marik and other drivel. On this night, he looked up and ahead toward the back of the bar, his protruding eyes never glancing at the patrons around him, those he considered waste and human refuse. As if trained to do so, his four cohorts formed a semicircle behind Marik, their hands out before them, acting as a buffer between their revered commanding officer and the inferior dregs of island society that might sully his greatness.

"You," Marik derided as he slapped the bar with his gloved hand, "Barkeep!"

At first Corky O'Brian didn't even flinch. In the scattering of years Marik had been on Motugra, he'd come into the Hanging Monkey perhaps three times, this being the third by O'Brian's tally. The two previous visits had been as pleasant as the Irishman figured this one would be. Like visiting a dentist sober and having no needle to kill the pain.

"Bar..." Marik stretched out the word as he raised his crop and prodded O'Brian's shoulder with it, "...keep. Your attention is required. I am here to meet someone...."

"How about," O'Brian growled as he threw his bulk around with all the subtlety of an attacking grizzly bear, "I help ye keep yer meetin' with five of me best friends?" O'Brian punctuated the caustic offer by shoving a pineapple-sized fist up under Marik's bent nose.

In an instant the chattering and clucking of the bar crowd died, falling silent like a graveyard, nothing but the dirty wicker fans humming weakly as they cut the smoke laden air near the ceiling. Marik's four lapdogs fell in beside their commander, two on each side, their hands in their jackets. As if he had simply appeared, Khuna now stood behind the two on Marik's right, his ancestral spear held horizontally, the shaft pressed against their backs. Just as quickly but with none of the grace of the islander, pilot Jimmy Dolan tripped across two sailors drunker than he was and nearly fell into the men on Marik's left. He brushed one of them across the shoulder, the weight of his Police Positive .38 pressing through his brown bomber jacket.

"Need ta take a step back, dontcha think, Heimie?" Jimmy slurred.

"Ye might listen to the flyboy, Major," Corky suggested, his fist still hovering in front of Marik's face. "The Monkey's no place fer soldierin'. Fightin' on the other hand...."

"Corky." Miko deftly slid into view somehow working her way between the bar and the enraged Irishman. Standing with her back to Marik and his front line, she said, "This is a good night for the Hanging Monkey, Corky. No need to mark it up, especially over this one." She gestured with a backward jerk of her right shoulder toward Marik. "Leave the storm outside, Corky."

"Listen," Marik said, his whiny tenor trying to sound silken and smooth, "to your precious drink pouring lotus flower, barkeep. She, like her people, has great wisdom." He leaned forward, his riding crop still pointed across the bar. With a flick of his wrist, the crop jerked sideways, poking into Miko's side, roughly caressing her left breast through her shirt. "And she," Marik said filthily, "likely has other talents I'm sure you appreciate."

The stinging slap of Miko's hand against Marik's acne strewn face rang throughout the Hanging Monkey, forcing more than a few ragged gasps. Marik bellowed, yelling something in German, spittle landing all over Miko's face, a vision of incensed irritation itself. The men to the major's left started to pull their hands from their coats, but found they could not. Khuna's spear held their arms tightly against their chests. The native had somehow lifted and moved the spear over their heads, using it as a restraint. Both struggled, jostled back and forth, trying to topple the diminutive islander, but Khuna stood firm. And neither one of them could do a thing.

Although not armed with a long spear, Jimmy Dolan, drunk or not, was one of the fastest draws on the island. His .38 nuzzled the neck of the soldier to his right. Jimmy belched loudly in the other one's ear, "Now pull your fancy little Luger if you want, Adolf, but Heimie here will lose a couple of inches if you do."

"Outrageous!" trilled Marik as a few of the Monkey's patrons let loose a chortle or guffaw. "Do you not know who I am?" His face contorted with near insanity, a bright throbbing blue vein rising up on his forehead. "I was sent here by Hitler to take this island! And I will!" His entire body shook with a maelstrom of emotion. "Here, I am Hitler! I am Germany!" With a speed no one expected, Marik's right hand dove into his own coat and returned to view with a Luger in its grasp, the end of its barrel planted squarely on Miko's forehead. He roared, "I am Motugra!"

The tension hung in the bar like the cloud of cigar smoke clinging to the roof above, cut only slightly by the sound of leather and cloth crinkling and hammers being pulled back. Marik did not react, however. He glared at Miko and Corky, his bulbous eyes wide, red veins spidering across the white of them.

"Not going to look, Major?" Grace Thomas ambled her way slowly from her stool, her usual observation post at the other end of the bar. "Then let me tell you what's going on around you." She stopped just short of Dolan and his two playmates. Leaning lazily on the bar, she smiled that starlet's smile of hers; topped by that expertly blonde coiffure for which she was known. "There's a whole passel of people in here tonight; you saw them as you came in. Well, just about every one of them, except for me and a few choice others, all came in here with a weapon of some sort. Most brought knives, others wore their finest in gunwear this evening. That's all the rustling you've just heard. All those cute little accessories are out and every single one is pointed at you. Not to mention the fact that even though I am an American correspondent, I'm actually one of the wider read correspondents. Not sure why, but it's keen by me. That means of course, Major, that somewhere in the world, someone who is over you in Hitler's harem might just read the wonderfully descriptive story I'm already writing in my head about this evening. Who knows?" Grace couldn't resist pushing away from the bar and walking behind Marik, her perfectly manicured fingers stroking his back teasingly. "Maybe even your Führer himself will glom onto my scribbles and see that the center of my warblings is little ol' you."

Nothing happened for what seemed like weeks. When it did it was barely noticeable, a subtle relaxation of an arm, a gun barrel pressing less against a forehead, and a look of sheer defeat crossing the face of a man. Taking advantage of this, Corky gently took Miko by the shoulders and said, "Move away, lass. We're done here."

Miko complied, although her most fervent wish was to remove Marik's head from his uniformed shoulders with her bare hands. As she moved, Marik lowered his gun even more, finally sliding it back into his coat. Cocking his head to the side to look around the dejected officer, O'Brian said, "Get 'im outta 'ere, Khuna. And don't worry 'bout his boys. Every damn soul 'ere has an aim on 'em."

Khuna slid over from his two prisoners to stand behind Marik. The spear, held in one hand, now prodded the major in the back. Khuna's free hand clasped down hard on the major's shoulder. Khuna felt the shudder of revulsion tremor through Marik.

"I am Motugra."

"Get your filthy hand off of me," Marik squeaked through clenched teeth. "Remove it or I will...."

Handing his spear off to Dolan, Khuna cut off Marik's threat by taking firm hold of his shoulders with both hands. Jerking him around like a sack of flour, Khuna dragged the protesting Major, spewing poisonous slurs and curses in German from his almost lipless mouth, out across the Hanging Monkey. Three men at tables near the front door were up on their feet, holding the door open wide enough for Khuna to fling Marik out into the torrential rain and face first into the mud in which the boardwalk leading to the door now sat mired.

Marik's four men stood silent incapacitated with uncertainty. "Boys," O'Brian urged, a double-barreled sawed-off shotgun that usually lived under the bar now cradled lovingly in his wrestler's arms, "Ye best seek the better part of valor, don't ye think?"

All four men responded by walking backwards away from the bar. Moving slowly, they quickly became highly aware that what Grace Thomas had said was true. More than twenty guns of all sorts and sizes had been leveled on them. Those who didn't have guns brandished everything from pocketknives to sword blades, waiting for a chance to cut just a chunk away from someone. With deliberate steps toward the door still held open by Khuna, the four men glanced over their shoulders as they retreated. One of them bumped into an old man who sat alone at a table, a short, slight man, sprigs of white hair hanging flaccidly from his rather round head. The man shouted something, almost desperately, and wrapped his bony fingers in the coat of the soldier who'd crashed into him. The uniformed man muttered something like "*Dumbkopff*" and swatted his newly acquired hitchhiker with the back of his hand. As quickly as he'd latched on, the old man let go and blended back into the Monkey's throng of boozers and carousers.

Each of the four soldiers kept their eyes on everyone in the Monkey until they were outside the door. Marik was now standing, his entire body coated in thick, viscous mud. He screamed something as his four men surrounded him, urging him without showing disrespect to leave this battle be. Khuna ignored the tirade and tugged the door closed.

"Wonder what," Dolan chimed, "the Kraut was spoutin' out there?"

"He said," a tinny voice that seemed to belong to no one replied over the once more already raucous crowd of the Monkey, "that he would get you all. Every one of you."

❋ ❋ ❋

"That's why," Nick Fortune surmised as he, Miko, and Khuna stopped in the alley running to the left of Marik's Reichstag, "I didn't get my very own deceased ape. That stepbrother to a hurricane came up while I was at sea with…" Fortune's brain caught up with his mouth and he paused. "With payin' customers," he resumed, each word carefully chosen. "I'd have been in the Monkey if I'd been on shore. But I spent two days battened down and battered about on the Fortune's Folly."

"Well," Miko mused, leading the two men down the wall of the warehouse, toward the back of the building, "you're tied up in it now. Here," she directed, stopping at the corner. The warehouse backed up on a dock of its own, once the busiest port in Motugra five or six years ago, all for about the space of a week. Nothing but the Hanging Monkey and the graveyard seemed to draw business for very long on the island. "Door's here," Miko pointed out as she grabbed the steel handle and yanked.

The stench washed over them like a fine fetid mist. Khuna forced his way past Miko, knowing full well what lay inside. Fortune raised his arm and covered his nose, wincing at the foul fragrances assaulting him. Two scents primarily ravaged their nostrils. The stale smell of dust and neglect, and the putrid odor of decaying flesh. Either way, the three of them bathed in the smell of Death as they entered the back door of the warehouse.

"Never wanted to know," Fortune gagged as he brought up the rear of their march down a narrow hallway, his Browning drawn, "what the inside of an occupied coffin smelled like. I'd venture, though, that it smells just like this."

Khuna, one of his slender leather hilted knives in his hand, stopped suddenly at the end of the hall, standing in the doorway that opened up into the giant belly of the warehouse. "Your venture," Khuna said gravely, "would be correct."

Miko and Fortune moved into the storage area of the warehouse after Khuna. The vast room was mostly empty, except for a few busted crates and the bevy of rats that scurried in and out of the wooden remains. And then there was the area in the center of the room.

It was set up like a briefing room in part, but it also resembled someone's hackneyed version of a royal court. A throne-like chair, mahogany with a carved eagle sitting on each corner of its back, sat at the center of several other lesser chairs around it. The three intruders walked up on the back of the obviously main chair in the arrangement. Set up in a half circle, the other chairs were all pointed seat forward toward the raised dais on which the more elaborate piece sat.

"They would," Miko concluded as the three of them moved closer to the middle of the room, "have meetings here."

"Yeah," Fortune said, "and some of them just can't get enough apparently."

Three of the chairs in the audience around the throne were occupied. Three people in brown shirts, one wearing a gray trench coat lying wide open, sat in those chairs. As Khuna and the others walked closer, they could see they had been men when they were alive, but were little more than rotting flesh and hints of bone now. A fourth man in a gray trench coat lay on the concrete floor in the back row of chairs, as if he'd slipped from his final resting place sometime since he'd been relieved of breathing privileges.

"These men," Khuna said, studying the three closest to him, "died horribly. Stabbed, yes, but look at the marks on their faces."

Fortune snaked around Khuna, following his direction. "Bites," he said. "Bites and scratches all over them. Chunks of meat just torn away. Why would Marik do this to his own men?"

"He didn't," Miko said; up on the dais in front of the chair with the carved eagles, she raised her hand, beckoning the men to come to her. As they rounded from the back of the chair, both saw what she'd found, another corpse in a gray trench coat, this one buttoned tight and proper. It was a man, his soldier's cover perked on his head as if it sat atop a point. Even though most of the flesh had been torn or rotted from his face, somehow a hunk of meat still dangled from its center, enough to give definition to a hawkish nose ending in a fish hook bend.

"How long," Fortune managed, turning away as the stench and sight combined proved nearly too much for him. "How long have they been here?"

"Weeks," Khuna answered, having found animals and even tribesmen in the jungles of Motugra before, long passed from this world and joining the soil in decay. "Perhaps as long as three months."

"This hasn't been here," Miko said, tearing something from Marik's chest, a page pinned to it, pinned by a small ornate dagger, "for three months."

His curiosity piqued, Fortune spun around and saw what Miko now held in front of her: a map. A map of the island, with a red X—likely someone's blood—marked at the high right corner of the page.

"Left for us," Khuna grunted.

"Yes," Miko agreed. "But why be so extravagant? And why not take us as they did the other three?"

Fortune laughed. "Because whoever is doing this knows you two. Need I remind you of the seven men who had no plans to die tonight until they met the two of you?"

"If any harm has come," Miko seethed, "to Grace, Jimmy, or Corky, those seven will not go to Hell alone."

"Good," Fortune said, taking the map from Miko's grasp. "Then it looks like we're taking a boat ride, kiddos. To the other side of the island." He poked the red X with a pointed finger. "We're off to see Motugra, the volcano and whoever the twisted madman is behind all this."

Tendrils of sunlight rippled along the ocean waves like a fiery octopus rising out of the briny deep. Nick Fortune slowed his rumrunner—truly probably his only folly, hence the name—as they neared the shore. There was a dock at the base of the volcano that had given the island its name. Some millionaire had entertained the prospect of having his own tropical getaway, one he would invite friends to and such, so he'd built the dock in the most awe inspiring spot he could find. Of course none of his friends ever got to use it because the man with the money, according to scuttlebutt, angered one of the more aggressive tribes on the island, not Khuna's people, and he and his wife ended up as dinner for guests of this particular band of natives.

"Looks positively inviting," Fortune smirked over his shoulder to Miko and Khuna. At the far end of the dock stood four armed men, all dressed in black, mask included. Light from the rising sun ricocheted off the guns they held, showing them to be well armed.

"Three more," Khuna warned, his eyes locked on the foot of the volcano. "Two on the roof of Motugra's leg." Both Miko and Fortune turned where Khuna's words led them. Like many volcanoes, Motugra was ringed with tubes, offshoots of rock and hardened lava that had formed over centuries of eruptions and activity. Jimmy Dolan often pointed out to guests in his airplane how the natural expression of Nature's passionate rage at itself actually resembled a craggy stone spider from above. The various chute-like caverns extended outward from the base like legs. "The other," Khuna advised, "at the mouth of the leg."

"Miko," Fortune requested, killing the Folly's engine as they prepared to dock, "cast out the mooring line." Miko nodded and walked to the back left corner of the boat. Fortune countered her, slapping his hand on

Khuna's back and leading him over to the right side of the boat, the railing facing their welcoming committee and the volcano.

"I have a feeling," Fortune predicted as he leaned his back against the railing and faced Khuna, "that our friend only wants the company he invited. Which means I'm not on the list."

"And," Khuna added, "he will do what he can to make sure you go no farther than here."

"Yeah," Fortune chuckled. "Fun stuff."

Khuna pressed a flat palm against Fortune's shoulder. "Do not worry. You'll not miss out on any of the festivities, my friend."

As if to argue Khuna's point, a shot shattered the cool crisp silence of the morning. Miko spun and darted across the deck, the mooring line vanishing inch by inch into the water. Multiple footfalls echoed off the Folly's hull as the four soldiers on shore ran in unison across the wooden planks and to the front of the rumrunner. Miko found Khuna at the railing where Fortune had been. He held onto the rail, leaning on his arms, glistening like black marble. And the only sign remaining of Nick Fortune was his captain's hat, lying on its crown on the deck of Fortune's Folly.

Unsure of what she was seeing, Miko asked, "What... Nick?"

As the first soldier to board the boat marched up and took Khuna by the arm, the islander turned his head just so Miko could see an ivory smile cross his ebony face. "Now," Khuna said, "for the fun stuff."

The cadre of four soldiers shoved Khuna and Miko off the rumrunner roughly onto the dock. Neither of the prisoners fought or struggled, both knowing that they were in no danger from these men, these uniformed couriers. To struggle or try to escape at this point would bring death far sooner than their mysterious host wanted and would defeat the whole reason they walked willingly into the trap he'd prepared: the lives of three other people.

As the soldiers led their captives across the rock encrusted beach and up to the open maw of the leg, the other three members of their company, the one at the entrance and the two—one of which had fired at Fortune—surrendered their positions and fell in at the rear. Walking arm to arm with Khuna so she would not lose him in the approaching darkness, Miko imagined that the tube into which they now disappeared was the tongue of a great dragon, black and charred, licking them up as one final morsel before centuries of hibernation. Adding to her image of being gobbled up by an ancient giant settling in for an interminable slumber were the incessant hiss of gas escaping from fissures ahead of them mingled with the groans of rock settling against rock and crackling like the joints of an old beast sounding off in pain.

The black shroud that engulfed both prisoner and captor was heavy, smells of sulfur strong within it, heat bubbling up, sweeping over them in waves. As they trudged forward, slivers of orange light sliced through the inkiness, belches of flame exploding from open crevices. No one missed a step, though, for they all had the same goal, to get to the end of the lengthy tunnel and to stand before Motugra. Seven of them intended to bow down and genuflect, two of them to save their friends and leave nothing but blood and rubble behind if necessary.

As they emerged into one of the many interior rooms within the caves encircling the volcano, Khuna was reminded of the trek down the hall of Marik's Reichstag hours before. This place, like that one, reeked of destruction and demise, but not the same kind. Marik's final resting place wallowed in decay and rot, weighed down with dust and dead men. But the expansive cavern that this leg of Motugra opened out into was obscenely vibrant, lewdly and loudly alive with the prospect of death.

Rivulets of melted rock spilled down the walls of the cathedral-like cave, ribbons of heated orange flowing amidst fields of black. The acrid stench of sulfur that had teased their nostrils in the passageway now fully confronted them, stinging their eyes and coating their lungs with soot and their tongues with the taste of rotten eggs each time they breathed. The floor of this vaulted room was little more than an peninsula extending like a crone's crooked finger out into a sea of gas and lava. Although the rock beneath their feet ran from wall to wall nearest the tunnel opening, that proved to be only a ledge of about four hundred feet. A jagged spit of rock fired off from the ledge, reaching into the morass of magma around it, maybe three people wide. At its end, nearly all the way to the other side, it expanded again, colliding with another shelf of rock, equal in dimensions to the one on which Khuna and Miko now stood.

"What is this place?" Miko asked, mostly to prove the vile vapors of the volcano had not robbed her of speech. Her eyes widened as she took in all that was around her. Her attention was drawn to her left, shrieks and screams riddling her ears. At first she thought it was children she saw in the ten or so cages up against the rocky left wall. Naked children. "What...?"

"Monkeys," Khuna said. "Cages of monkeys."

Instinctively nodding her understanding, Miko swerved her head around to the right, to a sight even more disturbing. Tables, not cages, peppered the right side of the cavern. Yet these tables, like the cages, held prisoners all their own. Men, naked, held to the tables with leather straps. As she searched for familiar faces and thankfully found none, Miko counted ten, some of them with their heads wrapped in bloody bandages, their bodies twitching involuntarily. Others were awake and screaming, yelling, crying. Miko swallowed an indescribable feeling of fright as she jerked her eyes away from what they witnessed. The screaming men sounded exactly like the caged monkeys.

"Is this Hell?" she asked.

"No, my dear," came the reply, but not from the ebony islander's lips. The voice seemed to emanate from everywhere at once, from the hardened fingers of lava that made up the walls, from the churning and bubbling magma flowing like demonic molasses all around them, from the rancid bubbles of sulfur that popped near their ears. "This is not Hell. Simply a way station along the way for those who wish to challenge what will be!"

Taking this as a cue, the four men who escorted Khuna and Miko off the boat prodded them with their guns, pushing them like cattle toward the ragged bolt of rock that stretched across the cavern. Khuna grunted, swearing some oath in his native language, but the brush of Miko against him reminded him of their reason for being here, and he fell into place behind the soldier leading the way.

The procession across the precipice was slow, but it gave both Miko and Khuna time to evaluate what lay ahead as well as what they had already seen. Again, Khuna's mind flashed on what they'd found in Marik's warehouse as a similar scene unfolded before them. Although not of wood, this room also had a throne all its own, hewn from the very walls of Motugra itself. Although most of it still resembled a rocky outcropping, great care and work had been done on the armrests and seat of the chair as well as on the carvings that crowned its upper points. They weren't eagles this time, but something simultaneously simpler and telling. Each corner of the chair back was adorned with a stylistic, carefully carved M.

Other seats were arranged in a crescent around the foot of the volcano-bound throne. Not chairs necessarily, some of them were empty cages, others wooden crates that came from Marik's warehouse, still more that were simply chunks of rock or lava heaved or rolled into place. Regardless, it was obvious that the man who called himself Motugra shared at least one trait with the dead Major. They both liked to be looked up at and worshipped.

The comparisons, though, between the two rooms ended there. An addition to this one was the five men lined up in front of the throne, a cordon of black masks and uniforms, each with the fancily scripted M on the left shoulder, and guns. Another twist on Marik's shoddy auditorium was the set of chains and manacles to the right of the throne. Set deep into the rock with railroad spikes, a line of eyehooks lined the wall about six feet off the ground, running parallel with another row about six inches above the floor. Heavy iron chains ran from each hook, a circular thick iron manacle at the end of each chain. And trapped within each manacle was a wrist or an ankle. Wrists and ankles belonging to a battered pilot, a quiet, yet defiant lady correspondent, and a husky hung-over Irishman.

"'Ell," Corky O'Brian blasted, his Irish brogue harshened by having to breathe volcanic fumes the last few hours. "Took ye long enough, di'n't it?"

"Only as long," Miko explained, "as whoever all this belongs to wanted it to."

"Quite right, my yellow hued lovely!" The bodiless voice rose again, rampant with a distinctive English accent. "I do enjoy this one so much more than the other damsel. So much more."

"Well," Grace Thomas hissed, "I'm sorry that being manhandled by junior Jerries and ending up on the soundstage for 'Perils of Pauline' makes me cranky!"

"No matter," the voice cooed, "you'll all have time to chat and entertain my men and myself." A cackle took over the voice, sounding more like a witch's giggle than the refined, though off-kilter voice it had been. "Not much time, granted, but time."

Again, as if following some unspoken command, the four men poked at Miko and Khuna, trying to drive them toward two empty sets of manacles and chains. Khuna once more uttered something guttural but did not move. Again they jostled him, two soldiers shoving their gun barrels into his back. And again, Khuna spoke, in plain English.

"I do not move until the one who wanted me here stops cowering like a child and shows himself to be a man."

"You will move..." began the soldier closest to Khuna, raising his gun high to bash the native's head. In a blink, Khuna's arms fired into the air, one hand grabbing the soldier's gun, the other wrapping around his neck, five tiny anacondas strangling every bit of breath from his throat. The man gurgled and flailed about, but it did no good. Slinging the gun into the flaming flow around them, Khuna lifted the man by his neck and sent him after his firearm, screaming in terror and pain until the sizzling of skin ended the bawling.

Before any of the other three could react, Miko dropped down, scissoring her legs out into a split position. As she pulled them back in and leaped back up, each leg slammed into the ankles of a soldier. The two men fell into one another first and then, instinctively pushing off of the other to get their own balance, assisted in their own deaths, each one toppling off opposite sides of the precipice into the lava below.

The remaining man swung around, bringing his gun to bear, but Khuna's fist struck faster and harder, destroying the jaw and nose bones of what had been a passably handsome face. The bleeding soldier mumbled through shards of tooth and bone and fell back. Khuna delivered another blow, this one flat handed to his opponent's chest, shoving him hard. The injured man collapsed, rolling back and forth in pain, holding his face with both hands, blood and tears pouring between his gloved fingers. He rolled one time too many, slinging himself after his three comrades into the molten stream below. No one—not Khuna and Miko, not the five soldiers in front of them, no one—moved to save him.

"Now," Jimmy Dolan managed through his own bloodied, swollen lips, "that's the way you start a rescue."

Khuna and Miko stood on the ledge now, shoulder to shoulder, waiting for bullets, fists, or at least angry shouts and tirades from the five men holding position before the throne. But not a one shifted his weight, stepped forward, and even raised an eyebrow. They stood stoically as if they were statues carved out of the ancient black lava residue that made up the entire volcano.

"See?" The voice sounded again, almost schoolboy giddy. "That was absolutely entertaining! Why, it is so exciting to see one's enemies, even those less than he is, fight so valiantly in the face of hopelessness. And," the orator rambled, "those four were of little use to me any longer. Much like the three you left on the other side." Miko wondered if the three remaining men that had entered with them could hear their master speak so lowly of them. "They do not meet my needs, no; they do not."

"If we are valiant," Khuna demanded, knowing something of what honor and bravery means to some men, even one clearly insane, "then honor us by clinging to this mystery no longer. Show yourself."

"Ah," sighed the voice. "Yes, yes, the mystery. It was a dandy, now wasn't it? I must admit sending you the expired primates was simply my own little touch of gallows humor, seeing as how all of this started in the Hanging Monkey. I dearly love a good game, but I decided that perhaps a more direct approach was in order. I am quite scatterbrained at times, you know, really difficult to make up my mind."

"But," Miko forged on, "you did not attempt to take us."

"Oh, dear, no!" Again, sounding more feminine, like a pleasantly shocked grandmother, the speaker said, "I am many things, but a fool I am not. And as I've been told, I was correct! It cost me many men, again the loss there negligible, but you two presented more danger and risk than any of the others! And didn't this work out so well, taking three and dangling them like bait before the two stronger, more deadly fish? Yes, yes it did, I think."

"Enough. "Khuna's single word rumbled around the volcanic room as if the mountain itself groaned, most in the room not sure that the two sounds didn't coincide. "You kill us now if you are able. But we go no further until this madness wears a face."

"Yes," mewled the errant tone once more, "it is perhaps time you know who you maligned so viciously, so carelessly, to cause all of this. No doubt mine are the eyes that haunt your guilty souls."

"Khuna…" Jimmy Dolan started.

A tremor played its way through the cavern, a slight one accompanied with the staccato applause of breaking rock and growls of angry earth, drowning out Dolan's words. Any attention he might have been trying to get was drawn to the throne as a figure stepped seemingly from behind it, from within the solid rock wall itself.

He was a slight man, a wisp of bone and skin draped in black, but not the nondescript uniforms his men wore. This was most definitely a design based on that of what Marik had worn, what the world had seen when the now dead Nazi walked the island without his trademark gray trench. It was completely black, however—pockets, epaulets, all of it—except for the rather prominent seal over the tiny man's right breast. About the size of a coffee saucer, it was a circular field of red with a single letter stylistically scripted and embossed on the field. A capital M, this one with no swastika as its axis.

The little man, one most would have based on his looks expected to find tending vegetables on an English countryside or, if he were not in his betters, collapsed in a drunken stupor against the back wall of the Monkey, stood out in no particular way. His head was much like a round ball of flesh with ears, bobbing up and down on a thin neck as he circled from behind the throne and waited. One of the five who stood stock still in front of the throne moved suddenly, his shoulders slumping ever so slightly, his arms hung in front of him only briefly. He turned, helped the old man up over a rocky jut from the wall, and into the throne. The lackey then, with the practiced expertise of a trained soldier, turned on his heel and resumed full attention. As he reclined against the ungiving surface of the throne, the old man ran needle-like fingers through long strands of white hair, strands that were scattered about his pate as if grown from seeds sown by a blind farmer, some marring the effect of his black clothing, adding an unintentional smattering of white.

"Now," the apparent founder of the feast said, his voice raised in a tinny shout, no longer coming from everywhere in the room, "look upon me as you wish, native, you and your exotic friend. Look on me and remember that you are to blame for how your lives will end."

"But," Miko said confused, "I've…I've never seen you before in my life."

"Shite and bollocks!" belted Corky O'Brian as the thin old man, his skin wrinkled like poorly dried leather, stood upright, his chest suddenly heaving, his shoulders drawn back, his round head red like a ripe tomato. "'Ere we go again," O'Brian warned.

"Lies!" shrieked the man who called himself Motugra. "Your worthless comrades dangling now like charms from my wall wove the same venomous lies! To not know one that you destroyed, one who you crushed beneath your frivolous words and drunken debauchery! You are less than human to not know one you have wronged so savagely!" He thrust two spindly arms high above his head, shaking arthritic fists at the craggy ceiling. "Prevaricators!"

As the echoes of insane rambling died away, Khuna with a voice as even as a calm sea, responded, "Like the island whose belly you sit in the midst of, I am nothing but what you see; no shade other than that which adorns my skin; no motive other than to live and die as a man; and no reason to lie to you or anyone else. In all the years I have walked this earth, I do not recall your face from the storm of memories my Gods have granted me."

"Years!" Motugra cried, his voice cracking with ire. "You speak of years, you damned fool, when all it took was one night for you and the filth you call friends to forever change my life! One stormy night in that hovel you call a tavern!"

"Now...look upon me as you wish...."

"Stormy…" Miko repeated, her mind seizing on the only way this connected to all that had gone on before. "That night…the night in the Monkey with Marik. But," she arched a delicately crafted eyebrow, "you weren't with him. Those four, they…."

"Died, yes," the gangly old man rattled, "died with that insipid no account Marik. You found them; I meant you to. No," his voice lowered along with his arms, the left one at his side, the right one out in front of him, palm up, fingers bent as if he held some invisible object in it.

"I was not with Marik that night. Not yet. It was to be the beginning of a glorious future!" He moved almost involuntarily down the jagged rough-hewn steps leading from the base of his throne. He was playing to an audience now, a scene he'd likely forced on his followers for months. "One Marik envisioned as his way to power, his light to shine before Hitler, but even more, my future! Money to fund the wonders of science I knew were my destiny to wrought! Revolutionary medicines and cures and evolution not even Darwin could imagine! That," he said, walking through the opening his five men made without direction for him to pass through, "was to be my destiny, one all of you destroyed in a smattering of minutes."

"You were," Miko said, understanding dawning on her along with a dose of bewilderment, "the person Marik came to the Monkey to meet."

"Yes!" Motugra shouted, vindicated finally. "I indeed was the person that Marik came to meet. But because of how you treated my future employer, he wanted nothing to do with me, with my ideas, my plans to save the world after that night! No, instead he tried to first ignore me, then kill me! But," Motugra slithered across the rock floor and stood directly in front of Khuna and Miko, "I proved too much for him. His beatings, his insults, even his bullets could not kill me. And as he had his men work me over, I worked on them, told them what could be their futures; money and power, strength and ferocity beyond imagining! I changed their minds, changed Marik's plans, and," he grinned like a white toothy jack-o -lantern, "I changed. I was the lowly scientist that Marik meant to use and abuse when he came to meet me that night. But I became something else." He dropped whatever imaginary bauble he'd been holding in his hand and again pummeled the air above his head with decrepit fists. "I am Motugra!"

"This," Khuna said, ignoring the dramatic self introduction, "what you are doing with those creatures in the cages and those on the tables. This is to better the world?"

"Yes," the knotty tree limb of a man insisted, shaking a still clenched fist in front of Khuna's face. "Granted, I had meant to do it the traditional way, introduce my work through Hitler's armies and then become known to the world through journals and realization of my great deeds! But that night in the bar forever destroyed the man I was. The man I am now still wishes to improve the world for all, but knows that can only be done by force and control!"

He moved from Khuna to Miko, his fist opening slowly, his knobby fingers reaching to caress her cheek, Miko deftly dodging the approach. Motugra's tiny marble-like green eyes narrowed but did not break their gaze on Miko. "The man I'd been sought funding for proper facilities. He would have had sterile surgical rooms, appropriate testing grounds, labs necessary for refining the discoveries he'd made. Discoveries that proved our primate cousins had more to offer than just humor in bad jungle movies." He pushed past Miko, walking out onto the jagged path between ledges. He'd forgotten them now, his eyes darting back and forth between the caged monkeys and the restrained men on tables. The three soldiers who'd been left on that side busied themselves, one feeding the animals, the other two applying some sort of liquid soaked bandage to two of the men. "Do you know," Motugra intoned, "that cures for all that which ails the human body flow in the very blood and fluids of those masterful monkeys? The man I was found that out and would have saved the world with it! But now," his voice, still high, lost the nasal hint and gained a razor's edge, as he marched back and pushed his way between Miko and Khuna, "I will use it to first rule the world!"

""What," Miko said insultingly, "with an army of monkeys?"

Motugra spun around so suddenly, startling Miko, now looming against her like a vulture. "No, my dear, although those beasts are in cages because I have indeed removed any genetic inhibition they might have to causing war and death! I have collected primates from all over the world and in each case have been able to extract not only what makes them docile banana eaters, but I have isolated the chemical compound that remains—that which makes them true animals—and have been able to introduce it into the human body!"

Again with a practiced flair, Motugra raised his left hand in the air, snapped his fingers twice, and lowered it. The five men standing stock still in front of his throne reached up in unison with their right hands and tugged the masks from their faces. Where once clearly human features had likely been, there now existed only misshapen faces, black pinhead eyes set into deep folds of wrinkled skin. Hair of varying colors, depending on the man, grew in sprigs from their visages and their mouths, pulled back into rigor like grins, glistened with blood-stained white teeth, each one sharpened to a point.

Miko couldn't suppress a gasp. Before them stood five things that had once been men, but now more resembled primitive cavemen she'd read about or, even more, a blasphemous blending of man and monkey. Khuna, his face grim with sorrow and anger, said, "You have betrayed nature."

"Betrayed it?" Motugra screamed into his face, covering his ebony skin with a sheen of spittle. "I command nature! These five men and the ones on those tables that survive will be the new race of Man that I will lead across this world! They are vicious, they are deadly, and they are completely and totally obedient to me!" His voice shifted once more, returning to the almost pleasantly twisted grandfatherly tone he'd started with. "Unexpected side effect, that. The compound I derived from the cells of the monkeys alters the human host that can survive the transformation significantly, but it seems to burn out any semblance of free will or thought! They will stand as monuments to my greatness until I tell them otherwise or until they rot away! Imagine, a world of people who listen! Who will be saved because I want them to be! That is what Motugra means to the world!"

"Funny," came a voice rich with sarcasm behind the aspiring despot, "I thought it meant 'island where O'Brian sells bad booze.'"

A whirling dervish of white hair and spindly limbs, the man calling himself Motugra turned, his circular cranium bouncing up and down like a rubber ball. To the right of his throne stood his prisoners…Corky O'Brian, Jimmy Dolan, and Grace Thomas… all of them free, their shackles hanging on the wall behind them. And standing on the far side of Grace Thomas with water dripping from every part of his body, his usually wavy brown hair soaked and matted to his forehead, was Nick Fortune, dangling a handful of keys attached to a thin circle of iron in the air.

"Don't," Fortune advised, "leave your keys laying around in the secret room behind your throne where someone who accidentally swims into a back door into your volcano might find them."

Words strangled in his throat as Motugra quaked, his body trembling as if it would become a miniature volcano. Snapping his fingers three times, he screamed, "Kill them all!"

As if each one had been released from some sort of unseen leash, the five men before the throne all lunged forward, suddenly no longer in unison. Overcome with pure incessant savagery, the monkey-like men flung their guns aside, their massive gloved hands twisting into fists or clenched like claws. They raised their noses in the air, sniffing, inhaling all the scents of those they meant to hunt and rend from limb to limb.

As the five of them lurched forward, Fortune, O'Brian, and Dolan all advanced from behind. Corky snatched up the uniformed beast closest to him as it worked its nostrils in the air. Shouting something he would later swear was in the ancient tongue of his homeland, O'Brian lifted the startled man off his feet and ran, as if carrying a football, for the edge of the ledge. Heaving his opponent over the edge into the roiling lava below, Corky turned, looking for another taker, only to find most of the fun already over.

Following O'Brian, Jimmy Dolan dodged to the right and clipped another uniformed thing on the back of the head. Shaking it off as if being bit by a gnat, Jimmy's chosen foe ambled around, its misshapen face curled up in carnal rage. Tangling its fingers together, it swung its arms like a baseball bat, swatting Dolan across the floor, his head crashing into one of the abandoned machine guns. Not to look a gift accident in the mouth, Jimmy reached around, grabbed the gun, and then rolled onto his back as his playmate made a run for him. Squeezing the trigger, Jimmy watched as the mutated form before him danced like a badly worked marionette as each bullet struck him. Swerving to one side, Jimmy stood as the body thudded to the floor.

Nick Fortune was fed up. With Grace at his side, he barreled across the ledge, fists cocked and daring any of the three others to come at him. He'd been nearly shot, would have been had Khuna not heard the bullet slicing the air and shoved him off the boat. He'd then swum to shore, wrestled his way through jungle growth and over rocky outcroppings, nearly breaking his leg when he fell into the hole, another leg of the volcano that, as he heard voices, led him to the compact chamber hidden by Motugra's throne. Anything these three man monsters had, Fortune knew he could and would handle gladly.

One dove at Fortune, gloved hands out to grab his neck. A swift roundhouse right to the head knocked the soldier into Fortune's left uppercut, ending his attack and laying him on the ground. Without slowing down, Fortune drew his Browning and planted a slug in the man's left temple. Fortune swung the gun around and fired, catching another one in the shoulder. He roared, much more like an animal than a man and whirled, only to catch the pummeling fist of Grace Thomas across his hairy snout. Yelping like a slapped dog, he spun, facing Grace full on. Too late did he realize the barrel of Fortune's Browning hovered just over her shoulder. The gun spat flame and lead, a bullet planting deeply in the deranged monkey thing's brain.

Khuna swatted Motugra aside with one hand and jumped into the fray as the old man gave the order. The man thing closest to Khuna also charged, setting his frenzied eyes on the native. The largest of the five, the man in black roared as he swept up Khuna in a bear hug, his arms throttling the ebon skinned islander with crushing strength. Groaning as he felt his bones begin to crack, Khuna wrapped his pistonesque arms around his captor, embracing the creature's head. With a shout and a violent spasm of his entire body, Khuna twisted the man's head violently; the cacophony of his neck breaking sounded like just another gunshot echoing off the cavern walls.

As the cordon of men slung their guns away, Miko knew that Khuna and the others would be able to stand on their own. Moving to protect their rear, she ran breakneck across the rock bridge and jumped high into the air as the three soldiers that had been behind them were all now rushing toward the commotion. Two of them went down with a spread-eagled kick delivered to their faces. Miko landed in a crouch behind the one left standing, one who had worn his gun on a strap. Slinging the weapon over his shoulder, he lowered it, spouting something in a language she didn't recognize, and pulled the trigger. Miko tossed herself to the right, tumbling head over heel as he strafed the ground with bullets. She sprang back onto her heels as she watched the soldier riddle the unconscious bodies of his two fellow men, a few more errant shots leaving pockmarks in the rock in front of her.

As the stunned soldier raised his gun to aim at her, Miko caught a glimpse of something shiny on his belt and then leaped at him like a cat from a cliff, claws extended and bloodlust marring her beautiful face. Crashing into him, she toppled him over, sending both of them to the floor. As she rolled off of him, her fingers stole the shiny-hilted dagger from his belt. Before he could push himself off of his back, Miko sat atop him, driving the blade deep into his chest, leaving his heart punctured, his life ended.

The sound of clanging metal and the caged monkeys screaming somewhere around her roused Miko from her hunter's fever. Looking around, she found the cages, monkeys jumping up and down, shrieking at the violence around them, shaking the bars, fighting to get out and unleash their own surgically induced furor on the world. But what was making them scream was the old man in front of them unlocking and unhinging their cages.

"Madness!" Motugra bleated as his aged hands tugged and pulled at the cage doors. "Madness must be met with might! Go!" he ordered the monkeys, slinging open the last cage he could reach and stepping out of the way. "Show them what I have made you! Suffer upon them the wrath of Motugra!"

The first monkey out of the cage, an orangutan that could have been a twin to the one found hanging from Dolan's propeller, sprang at Motugra, its hairy arms wrapping about his thin frame as the monkey screeched in his face. Another smaller monkey followed by jumping and lighting on the man's hair-deprived scalp, sinking its teeth deep into the bare skin. Motugra screamed, but that scream melted into the gurgling laughter of true insanity as every monkey he released swarmed on him—tearing, ripping, biting, clawing—killing the one who'd made them as they were, the one who had corrupted them.

Tearing her eyes from the carnage, Miko lifted the machine gun the dead soldier she now loomed over had used. Standing, she readied the gun and, taking a steady breath, began firing into the multitude of monkeys. Most fell away like dead leaves from a tree. Three or four, though, avoided the shots and jumped at her. They fell from the air before ever reaching her, not because of her shots, but because of those that came from behind her. With all of the murderous monkeys dead, Miko turned and saw Nick Fortune and Jimmy Dolan now on her side of the ledge, guns out and smoking, with Grace, Corky, and Khuna behind them.

They all looked at the scattered bodies of monkeys, leading like a bloody trail to what was left of the man none of them knew by any other name than Motugra. He hung haphazardly from two of the cages, his left arm caught on top of one, the right tangled inside of another somehow, a spider monkey corpse clasped on his hand, its teeth forever sunk into his bony appendage. His parchment-like skin hung in shreds from his face, his uniform also in tatters. Blood poured down his body, hints of vein and muscle exposed where his test subjects had taken their toll.

"All of this," Grace said quietly, unable to hide her total disgust, "horror and waste. That's all this is. And for nothing."

"Most of life," O'Brian responded, "is for naught, Gracie. Some people, though, even louse up the moments that aren't."

"The Folly's at the dock," Fortune said, already walking toward the tunnel that Miko and Khuna had been led down earlier. "Anybody that doesn't want to walk back to the Monkey is welcome to ride." He grinned devilishly. "No charge."

As Nick finished and Corky, Grace, Jimmy, and Miko followed him, the cavern that had played stage to this debacle of avarice and lunacy trembled violently. The throne over on the second ledge crumbled as if built from sand into a pile as the tremor rocked the entire volcano, whole slivers of hanging lava cracking and raining from above. Quickening her step, Miko looked back and saw that Khuna had moved no further than the makeshift surgical area and the men, all unconscious or incoherent, trapped there.

"Khuna…" Miko began.

"Go," Khuna requested firmly. He now held two of the slender shafts of steel wrapped at their base in leather as he looked first at Miko, then at the only men left somewhat alive in the room. "The island prepares to restore balance to herself," Khuna said. "And to be certain there is balance, I will help her."

The End

WRITING "MOTUGRA'S REVENGE"

When the concept behind "Tales from the Hanging Monkey" was first dangled before me, I of course had the same flashbacks to the early 1980s that I'm sure others did. My mind tumbled back to *Tales of the Gold Monkey* and my amazement at how awesome that show was, even if it was a pale attempt to riff on the 'Indiana Jones' trend. As a matter of fact, that very reason is why I was also disappointed by the show. Not that it imitated *Raiders of the Lost Ark*, but that it never really pushed the envelope and went totally over the line into just *that* type of story. Oh, of course I now understand that it was cancelled and never got the chance to go much of anywhere, but I can remember being a kid watching Jake Cutter and company and just thinking, "If I was writing this, oh the places they'd go."

Well, I got a chance to write in that realm of Pulp with this tale and boy, oh the places we went.

The canvas of characters to paint stories from for this collection was rich and vibrant just on the pages of the concept bible. Every single person designed by Billy Craig screamed to be in whatever story I wrote and so they each are, even if it's only briefly. When writing a story with an ensemble cast, especially one with so much volcanic potential as this one, it is sometimes hard to decide how much focus to put on which character. Oddly enough, I didn't have that issue this time around.

I knew I wanted there to be a mystery at the center of "Motugra's Revenge." Sure, it evolves or devolves, whichever way you want to perceive it—but pure over the top Pulp by the end—but I wanted the reader to get wrapped up in questions and clues for the first half or so. I also wanted the mystery to be somewhat organic, to sprout on the first page from the middle and grow both backward and forward as the action progressed. The last thing I wanted to make sure of was that my "detectives," such as they were, were members of this illustrious cast already provided. Sure, I could have introduced an intrepid island gendarme instead of tipping my hat to Lee Marvin's Gilhooley from "Donovan's Reef," a local cop who could have tracked clues and tied up all the loose ends. But that's expected, that's normal…that's not where this story needed to go.

Of all the characters, the one most like the characters I tend to write was Nick Fortune. Although I included him in a pretty pivotal role, I worked diligently not to allow him to be the focal point. I wanted this story to be about identity on so many levels, including defining identity. To that end, I put Khuna and Miko at the top of my list to be the major protagonists. Although they sprouted to my brain fully formed, these two had a minimum of information provided about them in the bible. I knew clearly what they were as far as characters and pieces of the overall concept, but I wanted more. I wanted to know *who* they were. So, the mystery was two-fold for me as a writer: make sure the reader wanted to read past the red herrings and hirsute corpses to find out just who Motugra was, and to see for myself who Corky O'Brian's right hand gal and this intriguing diminutive island bouncer really were.

Here's a tip of Fortune's captain's hat and a hope that I did just that.

TOMMY HANCOCK has been told more than once he was displaced, a man definitely born a few decades too late. He is also a Pulp fan. No doubt about that, not since he was knee high to a flea market table where he saw his first ever Pulp magazine. Since that auspicious day, Tommy has gone beyond simple fandom. A partner and Editor-in-Chief of Pro Se Productions (www.prosepulp.com), Tommy has been responsible for working with writers and artists to produce New Pulp books and magazines since August 2010. An author himself, Tommy has written for Airship 27, Age of Adventure, Pulpwork Press, and his very own Pro Se. He is also working on stories for Moonstone, where he also edits and works as Promotions and Marketing Coordinator, and Radio Archives, where he also functions in a couple of capacities. Tommy is one of the Spectacled Seven behind ALL PULP (www.allpulp.blogspot.com) and a founder of the New Pulp Movement (www.newpulpfiction.com). Tommy is also Coordinator and founder of Pulp Ark, the Official New Pulp Convention. Most of all, however, Tommy is a husband who doesn't deserve his wonderfully tolerant wife, Lisa, and is a man blessed with three of God's most precious angels, Braeden, Alex, and Kailee.

"THE KNOBLOCH COLLECTION ASSIGNMENT"

By Derrick Ferguson

The radio rested on a plain wooden table near the windows looking out over the darkened street. Located in San Francisco, it was just one of hundreds of thousands of office buildings in many cities not only all over the country but all over the world. In these buildings there were offices set up for one reason and one reason only: so that instructions could be relayed to a very special individual.

Most of this particular building was empty, this being ten-thirty at night. Only a few late workers and the cleaning crew occupied the building. The night security men who were supposed to watch the lobby were in the storeroom with the night manager getting in a quick game of poker.

The office door opened quickly. The hallway was darkened, as the lights were always turned off on the floors that were not being used. The man who entered the office did not turn on any lights. He didn't need them.

He found the radio with such ease that if there had been any observers they might have thought the man could actually see in the dark. He slipped on a pair of earphones, settled them comfortably on his head. He turned on the radio, waited a few minutes for it to warm up. He adjusted the frequency to get a clearer signal and picked up the microphone, speaking in a low voice of power that was clear but could not have been heard from four feet away, so total was his control over it.

"Magician calling Intelligence One. Magician calling Intelligence One." The man who called himself Magician waited. As per standard operating procedure, he would give Intelligence One two minutes to respond. If there was no response he would leave the radio and the building and then disappear. Provisions had been made for him. He would go to a blueberry farm in Collinsport, Maine, and dig up a waterproof metal box containing fifty thousand dollars. He would then change his name and leave the country. He would have to. Because if Intelligence One failed to respond, that could only mean that Intelligence One was dead.

He hoped that would never happen.

"Intelligence One here, Magician. Repeat. Intelligence One here. Prepare for code of the day identification."

"Ready."

" 'The further off from England the nearer is to France-' "

" '-then turn not pale, beloved snail, but come and join the dance.' "

"Code of the day identification confirmed. How have you been, Magician?"

"Quite well, sir. And you?"

"Fine. Just fine. Ready for a new assignment?"

"Always, sir."

"You ever hear of Motugra?"

"No, sir."

"Not surprised. No real reason why you should have. I've only become aware of the place's existence twelve days ago and in that time I've become an expert on it. You will too."

"I take it I'm going there."

"You take it right, Magician. Motugra's an island in the South Seas. The seaport's fairly busy and getting busier. As a neutral there's a lot of international traffic passing through there and that's what we're interested in."

"What's the assignment?"

"You ever hear of The Knobloch Collection?"

Now here was something that The Magician *did* know. "A series of paintings done by Josef Knobloch, a contemporary German painter of some renown in his own country who has steadily been getting international recognition. Especially since he's finished The Knobloch Collection. a series of twelve paintings depicting the life of a man from birth to death. Took Knobloch twelve years to do the paintings. One a year. He has done no other paintings since he started The Collection and he will not allow them to be sold individually. They must all be sold as a group."

Intelligence One chuckled. "Very good, Magician."

"What I don't know is why he hasn't sold the paintings. They've been shown at art galleries all over the world and he could easily get millions for them."

"Knobloch inherited millions. He's not hurting for money. And there's a very good reason why he hasn't sold them. He was waiting for the right time. And that time is now."

"I don't follow you, sir."

"Knobloch's a spy, working for the current German government. Has been for years. As such, he's amassed quite a bit of classified information. Information that is contained in those portraits. Problem is we don't know which one or how many."

"You could just destroy the entire set."

"Correction, Magician. *You* can destroy the entire set. The Collection is currently in the hold of *The Vienna Queen* on its way to America for auction. Intelligence agents from all over the world are coming here to bid on the Collection and its secrets."

"What secrets are those, sir?"

"Secrets particularly damaging to our British friends. You need know no more than that."

"Where does Motugra fit into this?"

"The ship is stopping off there to pick up General Walter Dross, his wife and his staff. General Dross is a high ranking German official and one of the most dangerous men currently operating in the espionage community. Our take on the situation is that he's to escort Knobloch and The Collection to America."

"Sir, do the paintings have to be destroyed?"

"What do you have in mind, Magician?"

"Sir, destroying them would be simple. But what we should do is find a way to discredit Knobloch and remove his usefulness as a spy."

Intelligence One chuckled. "Handle it as you see fit, Magician. There will be a complete mission packet waiting for you at Harry's Diner on Drake Street. That's all. Good luck. Intelligence One out."

The Magician cut off the radio and took off the headphones. There would be no more communication with Intelligence One until the mission was completed.

The door of the office opened and closed swiftly. And just like that, The Magician was gone.

The Vienna Queen's passengers were at last cleared to disembark from the vessel and no one was happier than the captain of that worthy ship. He had not been allowed to let his passengers disembark until he had paid an unreasonable amount of taxes and fees for the single day he would be there. But that was Motugra for you. If you didn't know anyone there, did business there on a regular basis, you'd get gutted like a fat fish. The authorities on Motugra were barely a few notches above being bandits themselves.

However, if one wanted to do any sizeable business in that part of the world, they had little choice. Motugra's seaport was the only one deep enough to accommodate the larger vessels. The harbor was crowded with ships of various sizes and nationalities. Chinese junks bumped up against American luxury liners. British freighters docked side by side with native fishing trawlers. French heavy cruisers nestled up against Italian capital ships. The humid air buzzed and hummed with a dozen different languages being spoken, shouted and profanely used. Despite all else one could say about it, Motugra's seaport was never slow.

Captain Parmenter of *The Vienna Queen* stood at the rail, looking down at the dock as his passengers disembarked. He gestured to his First Mate. "There's a lad I'll not be sorry to see go."

The man in question was shouting at another man. This second man was desperately trying to organize the first man's luggage. There had to be at least two dozen bags, valises, grips and steamer trunks of various sizes.

"That's Gregory Duquesne, isn't it, sir? I saw him a couple of times during the trip but didn't really get to talk with him much."

The Captain nodded. "Be glad you didn't. Duquesne used to be quite the hunter and adventurer. Wasn't anyplace he hadn't been or anything he hadn't hunted. Man's a drunken blowhard these days. Rambles on and on and on about his salad days. Pity."

"What happened?"

"Damn fool took a bet that he could fight a bull over in Portugal. Probably was drunk when he made the bet. Well, you can guess what happened. Duquesne got gored pretty badly. Was in hospital for six months. When he got out he took up a new career: drinking."

"Being gored by a bull would cause any man to take up the bottle, sir."

"I suppose so. Still a shame, though. I've heard stories about the chap from men I know who don't exaggerate and let me tell you, Duquesne was a real fireball once."

"Who's the black fellow he's berating so enthusiastically, sir?"

"His valet, Alcatraz. Seems a capable chap. Manages to keep Duquesne looking fit, sober and neat at all times at any rate. Does for him quite well, I hear." The Captain shook his head. "Duquesne doesn't need to bellow at the chap in such a manner. Man's doing the best he can with all that baggage."

The valet did indeed seem to have sorted out the situation quite well by the simple expedient means of engaging several natives who obviously hung around the docks looking for just such work. Shortly, Gregory Duquesne, his valet and a small caravan of island natives wended their way through the mob of dockworkers, disembarking and embarking passengers, shifty-eyed conmen, sharper eyed thieves, harlots and sailors, heading for the most prominent establishment on the waterfront: the Hanging Monkey bar.

Gregory turned, an expression of utter irritability on his long, handsome face. Gregory Duquesne prided himself on being impeccably groomed, and he looked as if he could have just stepped out of New York's fabled Cobalt Club or The Baltimore Gun Club. His tailored summer weight linen suit had nary a wrinkle and one could have cut salami with the creases in his pants legs. "Really, Alcatraz, cawn't you hurry these lads along? I'm sure it must be five p.m. somewhere in the world and you know how I hate being late for cocktails."

"They're moving along just as fast as they can, Mr. Duquesne, sir." The valet, a black man in his early thirties squinted out at the world through the thick lenses of horn-rimmed glasses. Of average height, his clothes were nowhere so well tailored as those of his employer. Just a little baggy here and there, his linen suit did not have such sharp creases and more than a few wrinkles.

The Hanging Monkey bar was an establishment of some infamous repute in the region. A two story structure that was a lot more solid than it looked; the bar was the town's unofficial City Hall.

Gregory threw open the batwing doors and burst inside with an effervescent greeting; "Good day, good day and again I say good day to you all! Allow me to introduce myself to those of you unfortunate enough to not recognize me! Gregory Duquesne, at your service and for my first act of generosity but not my last, I'd like to buy the bar a round of drinks!"

That most certainly got the attention of the dozen or so regulars who made the bar their second home and they bellied up to the long polished mahogany bar that was the pride and joy of the bar's owner. Legend had it the bar was from the renowned Midnight Star Saloon that had been located in the town of Silverado in the United States. The owner had bought it years ago and had it shipped over to Motugra in one piece and then built the bar around it. Like so many other stories on Motugra, nobody knew whether it was true. But if nothing else, it made for entertaining speculation while drinks were being poured and consumed.

The natives carrying Gregory's luggage trooped in, grumbling slightly under their breath, but their eyes gleamed upon seeing the valet pull out a money clip bulging with American and British currency.

"'Ere now, what's all this, then?" A powerfully built six-footer with a formidable thatch of red hair came from around the bar. The once white undershirt he wore stretched to bursting across his chest. He dried his hands on his apron so stained and soiled it was impossible to tell what its original color had been. "Name's Corky O'Brian and this here's me place. Who be ye and what can I do for ye?"

The valet bowed slightly. "My name is Alcatraz Brown, sir. I am the valet of Mr. Gregory Duquesne. I trust you received the wire I sent you inquiring about the possibility of lodging here for a few days until we can book passage on another ship?"

"Oh, yeah!" Corky reached into a back pocket, removed a number of papers he had folded up and stuck in there for safekeeping. He selected the one he wanted and opened it up. "Got it right here. That your Mr. Duquesne?"

Gregory was in the center of a circle of newfound friends. Drinks were drunk as fast as the Chinese barmaid could pour them.

"Yes, that is indeed Mr. Duquesne, sir."

"Looks like your master might not be used to th' accommodations I provide here. We ain't fancy on Motugra. Silk sheets and champagne breakfasts ain't to be had here."

"I assure you, sir, that both Mr. Duquesne and I are accustomed to rough living. We're not looking for extra treatment."

Corky hardly paid attention to what Alcatraz was saying. His eyes were on the impressive wad of bills in the money clip. "I'm sure we'll all get along. How long did you say you were staying?"

Alcatraz peeled off several bills and pressed them into Corky's hand. "I didn't. But let's say a week, shall we, sir?"

"Sure." But Corky kept his hand out until Alcatraz had laid a few more bills in his palm to keep the others company. Satisfied for now, Corky stowed the bills away and jerked a thick thumb over his shoulder. "I keep some bungalows out back. You can take the first one on the right. It's one of the bigger ones. Separate bedrooms an' all." Corky cocked an eye at Alcatraz. "Unless your master don't want you sleepin' in the same house wit' him?"

"Oh, no, sir. Mr. Duquesne would prefer that I be close so that I can service him if he should need something during the night."

"Whatever." Corky gestured at the natives. "Whatcha waitin' on, then? Take them bags out back! You know th' way, ya lazy gits!"

Seeing that Corky was going to take over the job of getting their luggage sorted, Alcatraz took the opportunity to look around the rest of the bar. There were many large round wooden tables the size of wagon wheels being put to good use, several of them by individuals who obviously were not native to the island. They were looking at Gregory and not giving Alcatraz much attention at all.

Gregory was loudly coming to the end of a particularly bawdy joke; "—and then she said to me, 'hell, this is Tuesday, so it's *your* turn in the barrel!'" His audience exploded into uproarious laughter punctuated with much knee and back slapping. Gregory gestured to the Chinese barmaid that another round of drinks should be poured toot sweet.

Alcatraz felt a heavy hand on his shoulder and turned to look into a face that might have been carved from a block of marble. The man attached to the hand jerked his head at a table in the back and said in a thick German accent: "You come."

Alcatraz meekly followed the German to the indicated table. Another man, almost a twin to Alcatraz's escort in size and expression sized up the valet with an expert, professional eye. Alcatraz's escort stood slightly behind and to the right of him.

"That man at the bar. The one buying the drinks. He is your master, correct?" The speaker sat with legs loosely crossed, drinking schnapps that he had brought himself from Germany. Slender, with silky, neck-length premature white hair, he looked at Alcatraz with casual dislike, his narrow gray eyes suspicious.

"Yes, sir. He is. Mr. Gregory Duquesne of the Palm Coast Duquesnes."

"I thought so. I actually saw him hunt once, in Paraguay. That was maybe ten years ago. What business brings him here?"

"That's not for me to say, sir. Mr. Duquesne wouldn't appreciate my telling his business to strangers."

The gray-eyed man's lips quirked in disapproval. "When you're given an order or asked a question, *schvartzer*, you'll answer it quickly and with civility. I—"

The woman who sat on his right placed a soothing hand on his forearm. "Now, now, Walter. The servant is completely in the right. You would not approve of one of our servants babbling away our business, would you?" The woman smiled at Alcatraz with her large mouth. Short, yet with a generous build, she continued speaking in a resonant, low voice. "What is your name?"

"Alcatraz, ma'am."

"Please inform your master that General and Mrs. Dross would like to have the pleasure of his company at dinner this evening. Nine o'clock would be fine."

"I will inform him at once, ma'am." Alcatraz bowed and walked quickly away from the table. Dross and his wife waited until he was out of earshot before speaking.

"You seem quite interested in this man, Duquesne, dear."

General Dross nodded. "With good reason, Marta. Intelligence reports indicate that Gregory Duquesne may be working for American Intelligence. He may even be the agent codenamed The Magician who has been disrupting our recent undercover activities in America."

"Ah! Then I did right by offering the dinner invitation!"

Dross gestured at the bar. "You did. But the way he's drinking he may not be sober enough to join us."

"Surely a man who drinks that much could not be a secret agent?"

"Whoever this Magician is, he's a man of cleverness and cunning. What better way to throw suspicion off yourself than to play the part of a drunken oaf?"

"I see his servant is taking him out of the bar."

Dross snorted in disgust. "Probably to throw him into a shower and then to bed so that he will be sober by this evening."

And indeed, Alcatraz had Gregory by the arm, steering him toward the rear exit.

Behind the Hanging Monkey bar, a thick wooden walkway a few inches above the ground was the path that led to a number of bungalows of various sizes on either side. Alcatraz helped Gregory into the one set aside for them, and Alcatraz noted with pleasure that their entire luggage had been stacked neatly in the spacious living room.

Alcatraz dumped Gregory into a comfortable lounge chair and stood back. He removed his glasses and stood up straight. The transformation was amazing. Before, Alcatraz had walked stooped over slightly, his shoulders drooped. But now, straightening up and squaring his shoulders, he miraculously seemed to grow taller by a foot. His chest seemed broader, more muscular. And now, instead of the blasé, dull expression that he maintained when out in public, his face took on its usual expression of confidence and intelligence. In fact, his entire body language was now that

"You seem quite interested in this man, Duquesne, dear."

of command and authority. Where once had stood a humble, soft-spoken servant now stood Alcatraz Brown, codenamed The Magician. He folded up his glasses and tucked them away in a pocket.

"Sorry to pull you away so quickly like that, old boy. But I need you sober. At least sober enough to get through tonight at any rate. You're having dinner with a Nazi spy."

Gregory Duquesne lazily folded his lanky legs and smiled up at the man who technically was his boss. Alcatraz certainly outranked him. For certain purposes both men had official military rank with Gregory being a Captain and Alcatraz being a Major.

"You've been with me enough to know that I can drink ten times what I've had today and still remain on my feet, good Alcatraz."

"Well, let's not put your tolerance to the test today, shall we? The sooner I can get this assignment over with the sooner the both of us can get off this rock and back to civilization." Alcatraz walked over to a sideboard and poured ice water from a cracked china pitcher into two glasses, one which, he handed to Gregory.

"I'll never forgive Intelligence One for sending me to this Godforsaken armpit."

Gregory sipped his water. "Now, now, where's the dashing, intrepid secret agent I've grown to respect and admire? We've been sent to spots just as bad."

"When we first started out, sure." Alcatraz walked over to the window and looked at the magnificent view of the filthy rear wall of the Hanging Monkey bar. "Maybe I'm getting as spoiled as you are, but I've grown to appreciate assignments in Monte Carlo, Havana, Mexico City, Barcelona. Motugra is quite the come down."

Gregory finished his water. "So what now?"

"I return to tell the General and his missus that you will be accepting their kind dinner invitation. You will go to dinner. Keep your ears open and listen for anything that we can pass on to Intelligence One."

"Where will you be?"

"While you're having dinner, I'll be busy getting on board and locating where the Knobloch Collection is kept."

"Speaking of the great artist, where do you suppose he is?"

"I'm hoping you'll find that out at dinner." Alcatraz finished his water. "Now, go dunk yourself a hot bath then get a couple hours sleep. I'm going to deliver your acceptance then wander around the town and see what I can pick up." Alcatraz took out his glasses. "And *don't* go back to the bar. After dinner you can drink all you want, but I don't want you getting blotto before you've heard what you can at that dinner. Clear?"

Gregory gave Alcatraz a three-fingered salute. "Aye, aye, sir."

Alcatraz smiled and put the glasses back on. Amazingly, his body seemed to deflate in on itself slightly as if he lost height and weight in a second. His face again took on that slow, dull expression. Alcatraz shuffled to the door. "I'se shore do 'preciate yo' co-operashun, boss! I shorely do!"

Laughter exploded from Gregory as Alcatraz went on out the door.

Alcatraz re-entered the Hanging Monkey bar and slowly made his way to the table where The Drosses still sat. Alcatraz stopped a respectful distance and bowed. "Begging your pardon, General and ma'am. Mr. Duquesne wanted me to convey his thanks for your kind invitation and inform you that he accepts. Where will you be dining, sir?"

"Tell Mr. Duquesne that we dine aboard *The Vienna Queen*. We are most delighted that he will be joining us." Dross replied. "He can leave you here. We have our own servants who will look after our needs."

"I'm sure that will be most satisfactory to all parties, sir."

The narrow gray eyes of General Dross narrowed even more as he wondered if there was a subtle insult in that statement. But he let it pass and waved his dismissal at Alcatraz.

That suited Alcatraz just fine. He wanted to go down to the dock and get a good look at *The Vienna Queen* anyway and plan out the best way he could get aboard the ship that night.

Dross watched him go out the batwing doors of the bar. "I don't like him," he stated flatly. He gestured to one of his bodyguards. "Follow him for a bit. See where he goes, who he talks to. Report back in an hour."

The bodyguard nodded, stood up and went about his job. Marta Dross poured herself a glass of schnapps and reached in her small purse for her cigarettes and her ivory cigarette holder. "Really, Walter…he's just a servant. What do you think he's capable of?"

"If Duquesne is indeed The Magician then he'll know we're watching him. He may be making use of this servant to pass along messages to another agent on the island. It won't hurt to watch the servant for a bit." Dross gestured to the other bodyguard. "You return to the ship, inform *Herr* Knobloch that we'll be having a guest for dinner."

The other bodyguard nodded and departed, as Corky O'Brian bustled up to the table, tossing a rag over one muscular shoulder. "Everythin' to your likin', General?"

"Yes, indeed. One question, though. If I may…?" Dross held out a couple of bills.

Corky made them disappear into his pocket with the skill of a trained stage illusionist. "Ask away."

"That man, Duquesne. Do you know why he's here?"

Corky shrugged. "No idea. Got a wire from his man a couple days ago asking could I help them out with accommodations? I did."

"That's all?"

Corky gave Dross a look that communicated even better than his following words: "yeah. That's *all*."

Dross plainly didn't like the tone in Corky's voice. But again that soothing hand from his wife decided the issue. Dross smiled with pleasure and said: "Thank you for your courtesy, innkeeper. That will be all."

Corky grunted and walked away. Marta whispered urgently in her husband's ear. "You'd do well to remember your responsibility, Walter! You're here to see that The Knobloch Collection remains safe until it reaches America!"

"You are right, as always, dear wife." Dross gently kissed her soft, rounded cheek. "I'll just be glad to be off this island. There's something about it that makes the hairs on the back of my neck stand up."

"How much longer must we stay here?"

"We wait for a ship to arrive with several important men who will be participating in the auction. Once they arrive tomorrow, we can leave the day after that."

Marta stroked the back of his neck. "There, that takes care of those annoying hairs! And as for the rest, everything will be fine, I'm sure."

Alcatraz smoked a cigarette while strolling along the dock. He'd been in many a grimy port in his career but few matched Motugra's. Almost everybody Alcatraz passed looked as if they'd broken out of a prison somewhere yesterday. Men and women openly carried weapons as if it were the most natural thing in the world, and they all looked as if they were more than capable of using those weapons.

It didn't take Alcatraz long to catch on that he was being followed. It was easy to have eyes in the back of your head when you took advantage of every reflective surface in front of you to check out what was happening behind you.

One of the German general's bodyguards tailed him. The man was good. He used the crowd to maximum effect, using it to shield him while still staying within sight of Alcatraz. If Alcatraz hadn't been expecting a tail and actively looking for it, he'd never had spotted him.

Alcatraz grinned to himself and abruptly dropped, pretending to tie his shoelace.

The bodyguard, alarmed at Alcatraz's suddenly dropping, shoved his way forward, thinking that maybe his quarry had fainted, unused to the nigh-oppressive heat and humidity. He reached the spot where Alcatraz had dropped and looked down in shocked astonishment.

Alcatraz was gone. The bodyguard turned around in a complete circle, ignoring the curses and shoves from the men and women he jostled. It was no use. Alcatraz had just up and gone. Somehow, in the middle of a crowd, in broad daylight, he'd just…disappeared.

Alcatraz stood in the shadow of a warehouse some ten feet away and smiled in profound satisfaction at the bodyguard's consternation. After a few frustrating, fruitless minutes of looking, he gave it up and stormed away, presumably to head back to the Hanging Monkey bar. Alcatraz resumed his own course.

The Vienna Queen was a handsome vessel. Some three hundred feet in length, when they used the term 'luxury yacht' to describe her, it didn't convey half of her beauty. Alcatraz's expert eye told him she had been built in Denmark. He'd been aboard similar ships in the past. He shouldn't have too much trouble slipping aboard later on that night and finding where The Knobloch Collection was kept. Of course, there was the problem of what to do after he'd found them. Alcatraz didn't simply want to destroy them. That would be too easy.

Alcatraz walked away from *The Vienna Queen*, whistling softly. For all the world he looked like a man just casually taking his time going wherever it was he was going. Certainly the armed guards on deck took no notice of Alcatraz, but he most definitely took notice of their positions and the weapons they carried.

Time to return to the Hanging Monkey bar, have a drink or two himself and then get ready for the evening. Alcatraz had a feeling it was going to be a frightfully busy night.

Gregory Duquesne gave his lightweight evening tuxedo jacket a final straightening tug and looked at himself in the full length mirror hanging on the back of his bedroom door. "You are most certainly one handsome devil," he chuckled at his reflection. The tuxedo was one he'd had made for him in London. Elegant and cool, it looked exactly like a regular tuxedo, but the fabrics of which the suit and shirt were made would allow him comfort in this climate.

Alcatraz Brown emerged from his bedroom, looking totally different from Gregory. Whereas Gregory was dressed for a night on the town, Alcatraz was garbed for more sinister work. H wore serviceable combat boots on his feet; black khaki pants; a black field jacket with ribbed shoulders and upper chest; and a t-shirt the color of steel dust. He picked up an olive green British Army surplus shoulder bag he used to carry items he found useful on jobs such as this. He also carried a .45 M1911 automatic. Alcatraz checked the ammo clip, satisfied himself that it was full and slid the clip back into place. Two spare clips went into his right pants pocket.

"You start banging away with that thing, you'll raise quite the ruckus," Gregory said.

"If I do my job I won't have to use it," Alcatraz replied, securing the weapon in his shoulder holster. "But it's also for your benefit as well. You hear me blasting away, it'll give you time to either get the hell off the ship or think up a convincing story."

"If I have to run, where should I go?"

Alcatraz passed over a thousand dollars in American money. "There's a pilot hangs around the bar. Name's Dolan. Supposed to be good from the scuttlebutt I heard at the bar. You find him and have him fly you off Motugra. Go to one of the neighboring islands, find a hotel and stay there. I'll find you."

Gregory nodded. "You be careful." He stuck out his hand. Alcatraz took it and shook it warmly.

"You watch yourself as well, Greg. And *please* take it easy with the booze, okay?"

Gregory held up the three finger Boy Scout salute. "Promise."

Alcatraz smiled. He cut out the lights in the bungalow. "Give me ten seconds, then you leave," he whispered. The door opened with no sound, and the shadow that was Alcatraz Brown faded into the night.

Gregory paused at the ramp that slanted upwards from the dock to the deck of *The Vienna Queen*. Several hard-eyed men were examining him with open suspicion. "I say, is General Dross aboard? I'm expected for dinner."

"I am right here, Mr. Duquesne." General Dross appeared, waving for Gregory to come on up. "Please, please come aboard. You are most welcome! Most welcome!"

Gregory did so and once on deck, Dross took his elbow and steered him toward the dining salon. "I'm so glad you could join us this evening, Mr. Duquesne. I saw you hunt in Paraguay, you know."

"No, I did not know. When was this?"

"Ten years or so. You were hunting jaguars."

"Ah! Yes…the jaguars were breeding at a horrendous rate. I was one of a group of hunters asked to come down there and thin out the population. Bagged ten the very first week I was there."

"I recall most vividly. You and that Russian hunter…what was his name…"

"Count Zaroff?"

Dross snapped his fingers. "Exactly! There were bets as to who would kill the most jaguars, you or him. Who won, eventually?"

"Well, that depends on who you ask, him or me. Now since you're asking me, well, *I* won."

Dross laughed softly. "But who *really* won?"

Gregory coughed theatrically and rubbed his throat. "Perhaps if I had something to lubricate this damned chronically dry throat of mine I'd tell you."

"But of course! And here we are!" Dross opened the door of the dining salon.

The salon was occupied by three others. Marta Dross extended her hand to Gregory, who gallantly took it and raised it to his lips.

"My wife, Marta Dross."

"Enchanted, Mrs. Dross. I'm honored by your invitation and blessed by your beauty."

"Oh, please, Mr. Duquesne…call me Marta."

"Only if you call me Gregory, dear lady."

Dross touched Gregory lightly on the elbow. "Let me introduce you to your other dining companions. This is Josef Knobloch. A painter of much renown in my country."

Josef Knobloch looked more like a haberdasher than a painter. He sized up Gregory with droopy gray eyes.

"Hardly a need to introduce the leading social realism artist in Germany today, General." Gregory clicked his heels together slightly as he shook hands and bowed slightly. "An honor indeed, *Herr* Knobloch."

Now Knobloch was interested. "You know my work, sir?"

"I saw an exhibition of your early work in France some years back. Your Black Fish period."

"Ah! You do indeed know my work! Let me ask you, did you—"

"Softly, softly!" Dross laughed. "You will have all night to get Mr. Duquesne's opinions on your paintings." Dross shook his head. "Is it not tiring the way creative folk will always fish for compliments?"

"If I could paint like *Herr* Knobloch, I'd seek out compliments all day long. But who is this marvelously gorgeous creature?"

The woman who held out her hand for the same treatment Marta's hand had gotten was indeed gorgeous. Barely over five feet tall but with a curvaceous figure that had been known to give more than one red-blooded male lascivious dreams. The way the bright lightning shone from her platinum hair almost seemed to create a halo effect around her head. Her kewpie doll features didn't go with her openly suspicious eyes, which scoured Gregory's face with the intensity of a Chicago beat copper.

"This is Grace Thomas, a fellow American. And a correspondent as well."

"Charmed." Gregory kissed her hand. "How is it that you stay so ravishingly beautiful in such an unpleasant climate?"

"Practice, Mr. Duquesne. Practice. Motugra isn't the first tropical climate I've worked in."

"Which news service or newspaper do you work for, Miss Thomas?"

"I'm syndicated, Mr. Duquesne. I find I get more exposure that way."

Gregory smiled. "I'm quite sure that no matter where you go you manage to get more than your share of exposure."

"What can I get you to drink, Mr. Duquesne? Or will anything do?" Dross was obviously well pleased with himself for the slight dig he'd gotten in. Gregory was far too wily to rise to the bait, however.

"I'll have an Allies Cocktail, dear boy."

The expression on Dross' face went from smug to annoyed in a finger snap. "I've never heard of that drink."

"No worries, General. I'm quite familiar with how to make one. You take one and half ounces of British gin, one and half ounces of French vermouth and two strong dashes of Russian kummel. Stir well and strain into a chilled cocktail glass."

"It sounds excellent!" Marta said. "I believe I'll have one as well, darling."

"Might as well have them all the way around, General," Grace said. "And what brings you to such an out of the way island like Motugra, Mr. Duquesne?"

"I just go where the wind takes me, Miss Thomas."

Alcatraz slowly eased himself to the deck, lowering from the open porthole where he had been listening to the conversation inside the dining salon. Gregory Duquesne had a number of gifts and one of them was the gift of gab. Intelligence One liked to say that Gregory didn't have a silver tongue. He had one made of purest platinum.

Alcatraz stayed in the shadows, making no more noise than smoke as he crept toward a companionway. His intention was to search the hold of the ship as that was where The Knobloch Collection was certainly kept. If it wasn't there, Alcatraz would have to find Knobloch's cabin and search that.

He crept down the ladder, ears tuned for any noise, any sound from the guards. There were three on deck but Alcatraz fully expected more to be below decks, possibly one right in the hold with the collection itself. Considering the value of the information secreted in one or more of the paintings, it was to be expected that there would be at least one guard there.

Hearing voices coming towards him from the rear, Alcatraz looked around for somewhere to hide. He lightly jogged to the turn in the corridor and pressed himself up against the cool metal wall. The voices got closer. Alcatraz balled up his right hand into a fist. He hoped to get the both of them before they raised an alarm.

The voices were going away as the two men went up the ladder Alcatraz had just used. They were probably the relief men for the watch on deck, which meant that those men would be coming down. Time to move.

Alcatraz made his way to the forward cargo hold. Not much was there, crates containing spare parts for the engine mostly. On ships of this type the cargo hold in the rear was larger and that was where the paintings had to be.

Once again Alcatraz slipped out and stealthily made his way to the rear of the boat. The crew's mess was unoccupied but not for long. Alcatraz heard voices in back of him, getting closer. He hurriedly ran to the end of the hallway, turned the corner and continued to the rear cargo hold. He eased open the door, slipped inside and gently closed it, dogging the hatch shut. If anybody tried to get in and found the door locked, they'd raise the alarm but that would give Alcatraz a vital few minutes to escape. He'd rather that than someone come into the room, catching him in the act. In his work his most valuable asset was his playing the role of servant and hiding the fact that he was actually the feared undercover American Intelligence agent known as The Magician.

The cargo hold held little cargo. The boxes containing the paintings had been stacked in a corner. Alcatraz made his way toward them. A quick inspection and—

"Turn around and get your hands up. Slowly. Make any sudden move— any move at all—and I take out a kneecap."

As Alcatraz slowly turned, he slipped a slim throwing knife from a sheath inside his jacket and held it firmly between the two middle fingers of his right hand. He raised his hands to shoulder height, palms facing his head to further hide the blade. In addition, the metal and handle were black like his gloves so that there was no glitter of silver metal to give it away. The speaker wasn't a professional, otherwise Alcatraz would have been ordered to turn his palms facing outward.

The speaker stepped from the concealing shadows. Silky straight black hair fell to alabaster shoulders. Turquoise eyes sparkled with suspicious curiosity and surprise. She was delightfully petite with a waspish waist. There was nothing delightful about the huge revolver she held easily in one hand. Maybe she wasn't a professional, but the way she handled that gun told Alcatraz she knew what to do with it.

"Who are you? What are you doing here?"

Alcatraz spent five seconds weighing his options. He could pull the dumb darkie routine and distract her long enough to throw the knife. At this range he could put it cleanly through her right eye, killing her instantly before she could raise an alarm. But obviously she was here where she had no business being, same as him. He decided to take a chance.

"My name is Brown, miss. Otis Brown. But my friends call me Alcatraz. And you?"

The woman's eyes plainly showed her surprise. "You don't talk like most Negroes."

"How many do you know?"

Amazingly, the woman smiled. "Not many, I'm afraid. Point taken." She lifted the gun a bit higher. "That still doesn't explain why you're here."

"Who are you? What are you doing here?"

"I don't think we have time for this."

"Yes we do. Start talking or I shoot."

"I work for American Intelligence. My assignment is to prevent the sale of The Knobloch Collection."

Alcatraz feared that if the woman's eyes got any larger she was going to rupture her eyelids. "This is true? You're not just a thief?"

"Ma'am, my arms are getting tired. Either believe me or not, but make a decision one way or another. We can't spend all night jawing about this."

The woman lowered the pistol. "I, too, want the auction stopped! I'm working with a group of German patriots who detest the political direction our country is going. We are working behind the scenes to try and do something about it! We've been in touch with American Intelligence! They promised to help us."

"My superiors said nothing about you or your group. And just who are you?"

"I am Erna Knobloch."

"You're Josef Knobloch's wife?"

"Yes. And it's vitally important that these paintings be saved! I can give the Americans instructions on how to use a specific frequency of black light to read the information that is hidden underneath the paintings!"

"How would you know that?"

"Because *I* designed it so! *I* am the artist who painted The Knobloch Collection!"

"So what does bring a big game hunter to Motugra? You never really answered my question earlier," Grace Thomas asked with seemingly carelessness. She appeared to be asking a simple question to keep the dinner conversation going while they ate their appetizers. Gregory Duquesne reached for the Shante crystal pitcher at his elbow. He had suggested to the waiter that unless he wanted to spend the entire evening mixing him drinks, he had best just mix up a martini pitcher and leave it in easy reach.

"Need I have a reason, Miss Thomas? I no longer hunt or seek adventure. But I'm too young to sit on the porch and rock my life away in my ricky-racky rocking chair. I like to travel and so I do."

"But Miss Thomas does raise an interesting point, dear Gregory," Marta Dross persisted. "Motugra is hardly Rio de Janeiro or the French Rivera. What could possibly entice a man of your obvious culture to want to come to such an out-of-the-way port?"

General Dross sipped his own drink while he examined Gregory with the precise eyes of a surgeon examining a cancerous tumor he planned to remove.

Gregory took a sip from his refilled glass before answering: "I might just as well ask why such a renowned and influential German officer such as the General is here. Surely a man of his obvious talent and training would be of more use back in Germany than here in such an out-of-the-way port?"

General Dross cocked his head. "You know of me, then?"

"Come, come, General! Such false modesty does not become you at all! And if I may be candid for a bit; your name *does* get around."

General Dross smiled with no humor as he replied, "Like yourself, my wife and I like to travel. We simply stopped off here in Motugra for a day or two before continuing our journey. Ocean travel can be exhilarating, but sooner or later one longs for solid ground beneath one's feet. Do you not agree?"

"I agree completely, General." Gregory drained his glass and reached for the pitcher again. "I agree completely."

The two drunken sailors stumbled back and forth along the dock, carelessly swinging their half-empty liquor bottles, singing "Sweet Adeline" at the top of their voices. Just two happily inebriated sailors enjoying their booze, the balmy night and their friendship.

The two soldiers guarding the gangplank of *The Vienna Queen* smoked their cigarettes and looked at the two sailors in amusement and a bit of envy. It had been a long time since General Dross had allowed them a drink. They'd been looking forward to some much needed shore leave. But General Dross had forbidden them to leave the ship.

The drunken sailors stumbled closer to the gangplank. "Hiya, fellas! How you doin' this evenin'? Y'wanna drink?"

The two soldiers swapped looks, each of them having the same thought: *Just a quick drink wouldn't hurt.* General Dross was busy at dinner with his guest and he would never know. *Just a quick drink.*

One of the soldiers waved. "*Ja.* Come on board. Quickly! Quickly! But be quiet!"

The two drunken sailors made elaborate shushing noises as they carefully made their way up the gangplank. Once upon the solid deck of *The Vienna Queen*, things quickly changed.

They threw their bottles in the water, reached for blackjacks. Within seconds, the two soldiers lay on the deck, out cold.

One of the sailors signaled and, from the shadows, armed men ran to the gangplank; a dozen strong, toting machine guns. Efficiently, quickly, with the silence of shadows they spread through the ship.

"Let me see if I've got this right...*you* painted The Knobloch Collection?"

Erna Knobloch nodded vigorously. "*Ja! Ja!* It is true! I painted them. But it is my husband who gets the credit. He is a man of considerable influence and importance. He comes from one of the oldest and most respected families in Germany. When he married me and saw my talent, he began showing my work as his own. He used my talent to curry favor with German Intelligence."

"Does General Dross know that you're the real artist?"

She continued nodding. "Highly placed officials such as the general know. But they do not care. In fact, they greatly prefer that it be a man who is acknowledged as one of Germany's finest artists and not a woman. Especially in the current political climate."

"I can understand that. Look, Mrs. Knobloch...if what you say is true, then that changes my mission profile. If I can figure out a way to get you and your paintings off this ship and smuggle you off the island, would you?"

"Absolutely!" Erna's head bobbed up and down enthusiastically. "Whatever I can do to help!"

"I need for you to go back to your quarters and act as if there's nothing wrong. Just carry on doing what you normally do. There's a bar ashore called the Hanging Monkey. You know where it is?"

Erna's snub of a nose crinkled in disgust. "I most certainly do. Calling it a place of ill repute is a kindness."

Alcatraz grinned back. "Yeah, it's a dive all right...but it's as good a meeting place as any. I want you to be there tomorrow at noon."

Erna frowned. "How can I? What excuse can I give?"

"That's your problem. Mine is to get you off this island. Shouldn't be too hard. There's always pilots or sailors in ports like these who are willing to do shady jobs if the money's right. I'll find one and make the arrangements."

"How will you get the paintings off the ship?"

"That's *my* problem. You probably won't see me tomorrow but you'll be contacted by my assistant, Gregory Duquesne."

"Gregory Duquesne? The famous hunter and adventurer?" Despite herself, Erna couldn't help but look at Alcatraz in disbelief. "He…he works for…*you*?"

"Listen here, lady…it's an arrangement that would take too long to explain and besides, it's none of your business. All you need to know is that I'm in charge. Now, we've already decided to trust each other, right? All I need you to do is trust me a little further."

Erna Knobloch smiled and nodded. "Of course. I apologize. I—"

The two of them fell silent upon hearing the unmistakable sound of gunfire from the upper decks.

"*Mein Gott!* What is going on up there?" Erna exclaimed.

Alcatraz motioned towards stacked crates deep in the shadows of the hold. "Hide yourself back there. Keep your gun handy."

"Where are you going?"

"To find out what's happening, of course."

General Dross did not frighten easily. He was a soldier, from a long line of soldiers. So when the armed men burst into the dining salon, he was the only one who did not cry out in alarm or leap to his feet. Indeed, he continued to meticulously eat his grilled lamb chops and pan roasted baby potatoes.

The four armed men took up positions where they could easily cut down everybody in the room without hitting each other or their leader, who entered the secured dining salon.

He was quite short with a feminine build and a pointed chin. Eyes the color of dried blood roamed around the room, briefly resting on each face in turn before coming to rest on General Dross. The leader made a respectful bow, clicking his heels together. "General Dross. A pleasure and an honor, sir."

General Dross wiped his lips fastidiously with his white silk handkerchief. "And who do I have to thank for providing this evening's entertainment?"

"Thurmond Smithingell, at your service, General."

General Dross smiled. "Well, I suppose if one has to be assaulted aboard one's own ship, it might as well be done by a notorious and notable pirate such as yourself. Your reputation precedes you, sir."

"As does yours, General. I trust that we can negotiate in good faith. And that there will be no heroics or ignorant behavior..." Smithingell was cut off by gunfire on deck. "...such as that."

"I sincerely hope for your sake that you have not killed any of my men." Although his voice remained as cordial, the look in the eyes of General Dross communicated better than any words what he would do if so much as a single one of his soldiers had been slain.

"I avoid killing whenever I can, General," Smithingell replied drolly. "But there are those who would insist on throwing away their lives." The short man shrugged. "What can one do? If any of your men have been injured or killed, it is on their heads." Smithingell clapped his hands together, dry washed them vigorously. "And now, to business! Where is The Knobloch Collection?"

General Dross picked up his wine glass. "You can have anything aboard this ship you wish. I will myself hand over my wife's jewelry. That is worth a million itself. But those paintings must stay on this ship."

"Not only will I take the jewelry and the paintings but anything else I desire. You are not in charge here, General. I am!"

"Half a mo', old top." The voice was noticeably slurred but still had an underlying timbre of elegant control and command in it.

Smithingell turned to the speaker. "We have not been introduced."

"Gregory Duquesne. Of the Palm Coast Duquenses."

Smithingell cocked his head to one side. "Interesting. I do believe I've heard your name when I spent some time in Africa."

"I've hunted all over Africa, true."

"I suggest you continue to enjoy your meal and leave me to my business, sir."

"Well, you might want to hear what I have to say since it *does* concern your current business."

Now Smithingell was annoyed. "While General Dross may have issue with my killing his soldiers, I doubt he'd complain overmuch if I put a bullet through your head."

Gregory shrugged, took a healthy gulp of his drink. "If you don't want to know about an American Intelligence agent on board this ship, fine."

Smithingell frowned. "Why would American Intelligence care about paintings?"

"Because there's information vital to both American and British interests hidden on those paintings. And American Intelligence has an agent here whose job it is to get the paintings." Gregory poured himself another drink. He'd easily imbibed enough alcohol to have laid any other man out cold. But except for the slight slurring, he appeared sober enough.

Smithengell's head swiveled back to General Dross. "Is he serious?"

Dross snorted in disgust. "Look at the man! He's obviously drunk. He's a well-known lush these days. You can't possibly believe anything he says."

"I can tell you who the American agent is right now!" Gregory pounded a fist on the table. "Yessir! Right damn now!"

Smithingell motioned to one of his men. He swiveled the barrel of his machine gun around so that it was pointing at Gregory.

"You have ten seconds to say something meaningful before I have you shot."

Gregory leveled an arm at Grace Thomas. "It's her! She's the spy!"

Gregory's mind wasn't as slow as one might have thought from all the drinking he had been doing. He'd have to drink a lot more than he had been for his mind to stop working. And now he was working on gaining time for Alcatraz Brown. He knew that Alcatraz must have heard the shots. The more time Gregory could gain for him by acting as a distraction, the better chance they'd all have to come out of this alive.

He just hoped he wouldn't get Grace Thomas killed in the meantime.

Alcatraz was able to make his way out of the cargo hold and to the upper deck without being spotted. The armed men dashing to and fro were more interested in rounding up the soldiers and ship's crew than anything else. From their shouted orders and confirmations, they had obviously been well briefed on the ship's compliment.

Still, he had to do something to distract them that he hoped would enable him to get off the ship and get help. Even this mud pile of an island had to have some kind of constabulary. If he could....

Alcatraz rounded a corner and came face to face with one of the pirates. The man gawped in astonishment for a brief second before doubling over thanks to Alcatraz's right fist being driven extremely hard into his stomach. The man's machine gun clattered to the deck. Alcatraz picked up the pirate and heaved him over the railing into the water which he struck with a tremendous splash.

He snatched up the machine gun and melted into the shadows. Excited shouts from the upper deck filled the night air: "Over there! Over there! Somebody jumped overboard, trying to get away! Shoot him! Shoot him!"

The luckless pirate only had time for one terrified scream before being blasted with machine gun fire.

By then, Alcatraz was already away, heading for the aft hatch. He figured it would be easier going that route than risk being trapped below decks. He had to get to the engine room—and do it fast—if his desperate plan was going to work. It was the longest of shots, true, but it was the only thing he could think to preserve his anonymity and get both Gregory and himself, off this ship alive. That had to be his primary concern right now. He couldn't hope to take on such overwhelming opposition by himself and once both the Germans and the pirates knew he was aboard they might very well both kill him then go back fighting each other.

The sounds of gunfire, curses and cries of wounded and dying men grew louder.

"You lying son of a bitch!" Grace Thomas leaped to her feet. "Lousy, lying drunk!"

"Sit down, madam," Smithingell said easily.

"But he's lying!"

"Is he?" Smithingell replied. "I think not. I don't see any reason why Mr. Duquesne would randomly accuse you of being a spy if you were not."

"There's nobody else here he could accuse, you nitwit!"

"But there are so many other stories Mr. Duquesne could have conjured up in his vodka soaked brain, my dear," Marta Dross spoke up. "And I myself have been wondering why such a beautiful and talented correspondent such as yourself chooses such a remote island to work her trade. Certainly there are more interesting and newsworthy parts of the world you could be, correct?"

Now Smithingell was motioning for one of his men to cover Grace. "I'm becoming more and more convinced by the moment, young lady. Anything you would like to say in your defense?"

Grace pointed an indignant finger at Gregory. "How do we know *he* isn't the spy?"

There was perhaps a dozen seconds of silence before General Dross, his wife, Knobloch and even Smithingell exploded into laughter.

Smithingell wiped his eyes and got his shaking shoulders under

"The luckless pirate…blasted with machine gun fire."

control as he replied, "Now to even contemplate that this man would be trusted to be a spy, even by the Americans...well, *that* is truly amusing." He gestured to his men. "One of you take her out, shoot her and throw her body overboard."

"Wait! *Wait!* Even if I'm not a spy, I'm still an American citizen! You can't do this!"

"In this part of the world it matters little what your nationality is. What matters is if you have the guns to back up what you say. I do." Smithingell turned to his men. "What the hell are you waiting for? Take her out and shoot her! This already is taking far longer than it should."

Grace pushed away from the table, knocking over expensive crystal and china that hit the ground with crashes that sounded even more expensive, screaming, "No! No!"

Temporarily forgotten in the moment, General Dross reached under the table for a loaded Luger that was always holstered there. Just a moment more and, while the attention of Smithingell and his men were distracted by the screaming woman, he would cut Smithingell down. Once their leader was dead, the rest of the pirates would be easy to deal with.

And that's when the lights all over the ship went out.

Alcatraz stepped out of the engine room and, from what his ears could tell him, his cutting off all power had had the desired effect. The highly trained and disciplined German soldiers were immediately taking advantage and turning the tables on the pirates. Alcatraz headed unerringly back toward the dining salon. The way he maneuvered without light would have made an onlooker believe that he could see in the dark. Alcatraz had long ago learned to use his other senses to compensate for such a trifle as total darkness. Indeed, his Final Exam had been his crossing a minefield at midnight, blindfolded.

Somebody stumbled into him and, from the burst of German that came from the man's lips, Alcatraz felt justified in clubbing him down with the butt of the machine gun. He continued on, his foot slipping in a pool of blood. He caught himself and made it to the dining salon.

From his shoulder bag he produced a small flashlight. He hated to risk it, but he had to see who was in the room.

The first thing he saw was the collection of bodies on the floor: three men, all of them have been killed by gunfire.

"Alcatraz?" The voice came from under the table. Two seconds later, Gregory Duquesne's head appeared. "Figured you'd be along to check up, old boy."

"What the hell happened here?"

Gregory stood up, holding onto the half-full martini pitcher. He placed it on the table and brushed off his suit as Alcatraz extinguished the light. "When the lights went out, everybody started blasting. One of the dead men on the floor is Knobloch. The other one is the leader of these bloody pirates and the third is one of his men."

"Where's Dross and his wife?"

"Scarpered. He was the one who started the blasting. Must have had a gun under the table. There was an American lass. Very pretty, name of Grace Thomas. I suppose she high-tailed it as well."

"I want you to stay here. It's too dangerous to go out there right now."

"Go do your job. There's guns here. I can take care of myself."

Alcatraz gave his partner a pat on the shoulder and left the dining salon. He had to get back to the hold with The Knobloch Collection. Maybe there was still a way to salvage this mission from the total mess it had so rapidly become. Now Alcatraz felt more comfortable using his flashlight for brief seconds.

He stepped over bodies. Some had been shot, other stabbed or hacked at. The pirates and Germans had made short work of each other, but Alcatraz still heard pockets of gunfire here and there.

And now he could see flashlights and torches on the docks. Somebody had finally decided to see what all the hell being raised was about. Alcatraz ran down the steps into the lower decks of the ship. He had to find Erna Knobloch and get her off the ship. He couldn't hope to get The Knobloch Collection off the ship now, but if he could get to her....

He turned the corner and collided with something soft. He rebounded, bringing up his machine gun even as a pistol was being shoved in his face. At the other end of the pistol was Erna Knobloch. "Oh! It's you!"

"Are you all right?" Alcatraz lowered the weapon. "We've got to get off this ship. Pirates are overrunning it, and they're killing everybody. And Dross is still running around."

"It's even worse than that. I...."

The explosion deep within the hold of the ship heaved it over to one side. Alcatraz seized Erna by an elbow, kept her from falling. He easily moved back and forth with the motion of the boat. "What did you do, woman?"

"I didn't know what was going on! I didn't know if you had been killed or not! I couldn't let the paintings fall back into Dross' hands!"

Alcatraz gave her a swift shake. "Just tell me what you did!"

"I found a case of dynamite in the hold! I wrapped a few sticks together, lit the fuse and ran."

Another explosion kicked the ship even harder this time. Alcatraz fought the urge to let out with a really good flood of cussin' and instead pulled Erna Knobloch after him as he retraced his path through the lower decks, explosion after explosion tearing through the hull of *The Vienna Queen*. It wouldn't be long before she was resting at the bottom of the harbor.

Alcatraz and Erna made it on deck. The dock was packed with islanders both native and expatriate shouting excited questions, pointing at the ship as it slowly sank.

"Alcatraz!" Gregory Duquesne made his way toward them, holding onto the railing with both hands, pulling himself along so he wouldn't slip and fall on the rapidly slanting deck. "You *were* planning on getting off this bloody ship sometime soon, were you not?"

"Here, you take charge of Mrs. Knobloch, get her and yourself off." Alcatraz ordered, pushing the woman into Gregory's arms. "I'll meet you back at our bungalow at the Hanging Monkey." And with that, he dived over the side in an eyeblink.

Erna gasped. "My word!"

"He's got to protect his cover, m'dear. Never fear, I'll get you to safety. And a word of advice: let me do the talking. I've gotten quite adept at covering for our Mr. Brown."

The interior of the Hanging Monkey smelled like smoke, even more so than usual. But then again, the entire island did, thanks to *The Vienna Queen* which had only ceased burning a few hours ago. Nobody had done anything to try to put the fire out. Everybody had just watched. On Motugra one took their entertainment where they could find it.

But now the bar was filled with patrons imbibing their favorite drinks of choice and resuming their favorite pastime: telling outrageous lies and making up stories.

Alcatraz Brown and Gregory Duquesne weren't in the bar, however. They were down at the airstrip, having escorted Erna Knobloch there.

She looked tired, haggard, but steely determination glinted in her eyes. Her dress having been ruined by last night's adventure, she wore men's clothing which did not inhibit her femininity one bit. Indeed, she wore men's clothing very well.

Gregory pressed a sizeable number of bills into the hands of the pilot who had been recommended and vouched for by Corky. The pilot hefted the bills, nodded and slipped them into a side pocket of his battered leather bomber's jacket.

"Aren't you going to count it?" Gregory asked.

The pilot smiled. "Didn't you?"

"Yes."

"So what's the rumpus? Corky said you're okay. That's good enough for me." He half turned to Erna. "Anytime you're ready, miss."

"Thank you, Mr. Dolan." Erna smiled at Alcatraz and Gregory. "Thank you so much for this."

"It's the least we can do. I wish we could guarantee your passage all the way back to America, but at least you'll be off this island and away from Dross."

"Indeed. And I will be fine."

"I think you will be." Alcatraz and Gregory waved farewell as she boarded the Grumman Goose which shortly taxied into takeoff position as the two men headed back toward the Hanging Monkey.

"How did Intelligence One take hearing that the boat with the paintings had blown up?" Gregory asked.

Alcatraz shrugged his shoulders. "As well as can be expected, I suppose. He said he would be getting back to me with further instructions. I would say that he has to confer with others before letting us know what to do next."

"You'd best go into your dumb darkie act, my friend. Here comes the beautiful and obviously furious Miss Thomas."

And Grace Thomas indeed looked angry enough to bit Gregory's head clean off. "Don't think you can hide from me forever, you bastard!"

"Good gracious, such language." Gregory cocked an amused eye at Alcatraz. "Good Gracious…I think that's a good nickname for her, don't you?"

"I couldn't rightly say, suh."

"You could have gotten me killed with your stunt back on the ship! What were you thinking of?"

"My apologies, Good Gracious….I was simply playing for time, hoping for an opportunity. Fortunately, one happened."

Grace eyed Alcatraz. "Who's this?"

"My valet, Alcatraz Brown. Say hello to Miss Thomas, Alcatraz."

"Pleasure to make yo' acquaintance, miss."

Grace's eyes went back and forth from one man to the other. "So it just wasn't a coincidence that the lights happened to go out just then?"

"It was one you managed to take full advantage of."

"You bet your beeswax I did, buster! While everybody was shooting each other, I got the hell out of there!"

"You would appear to be a highly resourceful woman, Good Gracious."

"You stay on Motugra long enough and you either learn how to take care of yourself or you end up taking a dirt nap." Grace pointed a long nailed finger at Gregory. "There's a lot more going on with you, Duquesne. There's been something fishy about you right from the start. I'm convinced you're not as much of a drunk as you want people to believe."

"I assure you, miss…I am."

"If you plan on staying on Motugra, expect me to be behind you all the time, buster. I smell a story. And my nose is never wrong." Grace stomped away from the two men toward the Hanging Monkey.

Alcatraz sighed. "Good thing we won't be staying. That young lady could prove to be very troublesome if we were."

"When will we be leaving?"

"I'm going to contact Intelligence One and find that out right now. Why don't you go on into the bar and have yourself a couple of drinks while I do that. Keep your ears open."

Alcatraz entered their shared bungalow and made sure all the doors were locked and the blinds drawn shut. Only then did he open up one of the cabin trunks inscribed with Gregory's initials. This one contained a powerful radio. He extended the antennae, slipped on the earphone and thumbed the microphone into life; "Magician calling Intelligence One. Magician calling Intelligence One."

"Intelligence One here, Magician. Repeat. Intelligence One here. Prepare for code of the day identification."

"Ready"

"Six Fifty Seven."

"Thirty-one"

"Code of the day identification confirmed. Did you get the Knobloch woman off Motugra?"

"Yes, sir. Just put her on a plane. A local pilot name of Dolan's flying her to one of the neighboring islands. She says she can make her way to America. I believe her. She's anxious to cooperate. Maybe with her help you can get at least some of that classified information."

"Well, there is that to hope for."

"So what's my next assignment, sir? When do Gregory and I get off Motugra?"

The embarrassed silence that filled the bungalow also filled Alcatraz's heart with a very bad feeling. "Sir? When do we leave Motugra? You *do* have a new assignment for me...right?"

"It's like this, Magician. There are people in both the American and British intelligence communities who were not happy that the Knobloch Collection was destroyed."

"But sir, I respectfully remind you that the initial mission *was* to destroy the paintings! It was my idea to discredit Knobloch and get those paintings off the ship!"

"I know that, Magician. And based on that I sold the upper echelon that you were going to recover the collection. There were a lot of people waiting to get their hands on it. Those people are not happy that now we have nothing. And Germany's not happy that Knobloch is dead."

"I'm not happy about that myself, sir. But that was the fault of General Dross!"

"Our sources say that General Dross has been recalled to Berlin where he'll be expected to give a full report in person."

"Sir, I request that I be permitted to come to Washington and make my own report to you and whoever in person as well!"

"You know that's not going to happen, Magician. Thanks to the illusion you yourself created and maintained, everybody thinks The Magician is Duquesne. Oh, there are those who say he's too drunk to be a spy, but they still believe that The Magician is a white man. This current administration would never admit publicly that one of our most successful undercover agents is a Negro."

"And that success rate should count for something."

"You are only as good as your last assignment, Magician."

"But the Knobloch woman! She...."

"It's just no good, Magician. I couldn't take you off that rock even if I wanted to. For the foreseeable future, Motugra *is* your assignment. Make the best of it."

"Isn't there anything I can do or say that will get me off this island, sir?"

"Pull off one hell of a coup, Magician. Keep your eyes and ears open and find me a piece of intelligence I can use to pull you off Motugra."

"And how am I supposed to do that?"

"You're the one codenamed Magician. You'll find a way."

Intelligence One broke the connection without signing off. Alcatraz allowed himself a rare emotional indulgence and filled the bungalow with an impressively profane opinion of Motugra, the Knobloch Collection assignment, Intelligence One and just about anything else that came to mind for the next two minutes.

He then put away the radio and returned to the Hanging Monkey bar. Somebody had produced a Cajun accordion and accompanied the bar's patrons as they bellowed out the words to "The Double Jointed Apothecary's Daughter." The version with *all* the lyrics.

Alcatraz found an empty table and sat down. He felt absolutely numb. He was no longer mad. In fact, he now felt not much of anything.

Gregory Duquesne sat down heavily next to him, a bottle of rum in his hand. "So what's the news? Where are we going next?"

Alcatraz Brown took the bottle and upended it, taking a good long swig. He sat the bottle down in front of the astonished Gregory, whose lower jaw simply dropped open in silent disbelief.

In his normal speaking voice, Alcatraz said, "Gregory…I think we're going to have to get used to spending our evenings like this…."

The End

Meet The Magician

Even though I usually whine and moan like a little girl when it comes to writing these things, it's not the case this time as I'm actually eager to explain why I jumped at the opportunity to write this story.

Y'see, while I've written stories in what is known as the "pulp" style, those stories have been set in the modern day. Until Captain Ron was good enough to offer me a slot in a Dan Fowler anthology and one in TALES FROM THE HANGING MONKEY, I'd never written a Pulp story set in what I consider an authentic Pulp atmosphere. Namely, the 1930's. I mean, I think that if you are going to be a Pulp writer then you oughta at least occasionally write a story set during the 1930s or 1940s just to say that you did.

I wanted to do a lot of different things in this story. I knew I wanted to have a legitimate black hero and have him be a believable hero in a time and culture where black men weren't usually looked on as being heroic. There's a lot a background to Alcatraz Brown, just a little of which comes out in this story. If I get the opportunity to write further stories about the character, more of that background will be revealed. I wanted to have more humor than I usually do in my stories. Hopefully, I do. If not, lemme know and I won't do it again.

Above all, I wanted readers to feel as if this story really was happening on the same island as the other stories even though it's not your typical island adventure story.

Knowing the other writers in the anthology, I figured that there would be lots of high-octane pedal-through-the-floorboards wild adventuring. I wanted to have adventure in my story as well, but of a different sort. A more spy-themed type of yarn to set up the part of the premise of the Hanging Monkey concept that the island of Motugra is to become a hotbed of international intrigue. I wanted to do a story with a little more set-up, so to speak, so that all the elements for future stories would be solidly in place and I can just jump in with both feet if and when I visit Motugra again.

Hopefully, along with the other extraordinarily talented writers in this book, I've done my job and you'll want to see more of Alcatraz Brown as he looks for that one big assignment that will get him off Motugra. If so, you know what to do.

DERRICK FERGUSON – I'm from Brooklyn, New York where I have lived for most of my still young life. Been married for 28 years to the wonderful Patricia Cabbagestalk-Ferguson, who lets me get away with far more than is good for me.

My interests include radio/audio drama, Classic Pulp from the 30s/40s/50s and New Pulp being written today, Marvel/DC fan fiction, Star Trek in particular and all Science Fiction in general, animation, television, movies, cooking, looooong road trips and casual gaming on the Xbox 360.

Running a close second with writing as an obsession is my love of movies. I'm currently the co-host of the BETTER IN THE DARK podcast where my partner, Thomas Deja and I rant and rave about movies on a bi-weekly basis.

I'm also a rotating co-host of the PULPED! Podcast along with Tommy Hancock, Ron Fortier and Barry Reese where we interview writers of the New Pulp Movement as well as discuss the various themes, topics, ebb and flow of what New Pulp is and why you should be reading it.

And now we come to the part where I blurb and brag about the books I've written:

DILLON AND THE VOICE OF ODIN and DILLON AND THE LEGEND OF THE GOLDEN BELL are the first two books featuring my signature character, a charismatic, daring and highly skilled black adventurer/mercenary named Dillon. Check out the DILLON blog http://dillon-dlferguson.blogspot.com/ for more info.

DERRICK FERGUSON'S MOVIE REVIEW NOTEBOOK and THE RETURN OF DERRICK FERGUSON'S MOVIE REVIEW NOTEBOOK are two volumes of my movie reviews. For current reviews feel free to check out THE FERGUSON THEATER https://derricklferguson.wordpress.com/

HANGING OUT
AT THE
HANGING MONKEY
By Ron Fortier

I am asked quite often what process I go through in choosing a title to produce for Airship 27 Productions. Naturally there is a particular pulp format we adhere to in all the books we do, no matter their specific genre. We look for well written tales with breakneck pacing and colorful characters. Those are standards you will find in all our titles.

Of course we also like to have fun and every once in a while do something a little bit different. Such was the case when writer Bill Craig came to me with the idea to do an anthology series that would be an homage to a little known, but much loved, TV series from 1982; a series clearly inspired by the Indiana Jones movies of George Lucas.

Now that alone would have been enough to snare my interest, but it was the second part of this offer that truly appealed to me; that being the chance to work with Bill. You see, I'd been familiar with Bill as the creator of his own well received pulp series such as Hardluck Hannigan & Decker P.I. Bill's a great guy and knowing if I went with his idea he'd be on board to write for Airship 27 was the major incentive that made this fly.

Lo and behold, then two of our most prolific regulars also signed on to do a story in this set-up. Derrick Ferguson and Joshua Reynolds are two of the best new pulp writers in the game today and have done multiple projects for us in the past. It is always a joy to have them along. Then came the next bit of good news, the fourth and final slot was to be filled with my good pal and colleague, Tommy Hancock. Up until this project, Tommy had only done one tale for us: a Virgil Earp story in our first Masked Rider book. Of course by now most of you know that one little old story ultimately knocked over a row of dominos that resulted in a brand new pulp publishing house, Pro Se, and a fantastic new pulp convention, Pulp Ark. Amazing what one little story can do.

I would also like to add that South Sea Islands stories had been a staple of the classic pulps as well and been around a long, long time. In 1946, famous author James Michener wrote a series of stories about his adventures during World War II which became an instant bestseller, "Tales of the South Pacific." Later, in 1959, ABC asked him to develop that book into a weekly television series about a Korean war veteran who purchases a 82 feet schooner, "Tiki," and goes off in search of cargo and passengers. His name was Adam Troy and he was played by Gardner McKay. Adventures in Paradise lasted from 1959 to 1962. Twenty years later that same network gave us *Tales of the Gold Monkey.*

So there you have it, my reasons for wanting to put out TALES FROM THE HANGING MONKEY, my fond memories of two old TV shows and the chance to work with four of the coolest new pulp scribes around. And if you've read through the book, you'll know why that meant so much to me. It's just fun hanging with these hombres and I hope we all get to do it again really soon. Thanks for joining us.

Ron Fortier
2/14/2012
Fort Collins, CO.
(Airship27@comcast.net)
(www.Airship27.Com)

Coming from Airship 27 Summer 2012